FEATURING STORIES BY

TUCKER LIEBERMAN
RYSZARD MEREY
ZILLA NOVIKOV
ROHAN O'DUILL
ANNA OTTO
RACHEL A. ROSEN
DALE STROMBERG

CONTENTS

PREFACE

Pity the creative in the era of late-stage capitalism.

No longer an artist, a writer, a musician, they have been relegated to "content creator," a lone voice side-hustling in an oversaturated field where ever-evolving technologies guarantee everyone and no one their fifteen minutes of fame. Forget about earning a buck producing great—or even mediocre—art. The only way anybody makes money in this racket is by selling the rubes a dream of a platform and a paycheque, joining the endless multitude of grifters squeezing blood from a stone by putting themselves between the story and the reader.

With a broken publishing industry dominated by an oligopoly, a distribution network ruled by a black box algorithm, and a chorus of tech billionaires cackling about how they'll replace the innate human storytelling drive with content generated by robots, how can a lone creative ever hope to find an audience for their self-expression?

The answer is: you can't. The game is rigged, it has always been rigged, and you have a better chance of finding a winning lottery ticket on the ground than of making a living as a writer or artist. But that doesn't mean that you should give up hope. Because a lone creative doesn't need to be alone forever. There are creative communities, and this anthology exists as a testament to what a group of writers and artists can produce when they work together to lift each other up.

Whether we come from the traditional, small press, or indie publishing world, the members of the Night Beats collective are tired of accepting the publishing status quo. We've brought to you nine uncompromising stories about the struggle to be heard. From the mythological past to the automated future, these stories explore what it means to tell stories and find your audience, even if you have to consign your soul to Hell in the process.

Rachel A. Rosen
Night Beats co-founder
September 2023, Tkaronto (Toronto)

Art is a Service: Publishing's Rise from the Ashes with Nao Hovgaard

Dale Stromberg

*N*ao Hovgaard founded UpWomxn Books in 2018 and has overseen the remarkable growth of a publishing company within a moribund industry. We asked Hovgaard, a noted feminist, to talk to us about womxn in fiction, his era-defining success, and what it all means for the future of the female literary arts.

***

R. *Woebeset Blackwell:* I suppose we should start at the start. What was the genesis of UpWomxn?

Nao Hovgaard: Wrong. That is wrong. You don't start at the beginning. You start in medias res. You need to know where we are now, not where we came from. The earlier stuff can be worked in as backstory, as dialogue, as flashback. Do you see what I'm doing here? Approaching this as story.

Everything is story, or potentially can be. You have to live and breathe this. You have to be a writer at every turn. I'm talking about the dedication to this art, this literary craft. And then what we do is, we turn around and we give people the very best of that, in a way that makes sense, where they're willing to, you know, where you can convert that into a sales experience.

Convert. Convert. That's our passion. You spread it, you get it to go viral, and then within that vanishingly small window of virality you have to make that conversion. So that's where we are right now. And, you know—I want to stay modest, but at the same time, it is what it is. We are doing well.

Blackwell:* By "doing well", you're referring to the *New York T—

Hovgaard: Fuck the bestseller list. That's a dead metric; it's just another fossilized remnant of an industry that doesn't realize it has gone extinct. That's what we're here disrupting. The fact that we laid waste to the list, it doesn't matter, because they're not even tracking the bulk of the sales that we're making, they're out focusing on these old-ass behind-the-times bricks-and-mortar... Ugh. It's like going to the fucking library. It has nothing to do with how people live.

Look at it this way. The fact we could rail that *NYT* list—like, rail it in a sundress, but sort of accidentally, like just with the fraction of our sales that they're capable of tracking—it just shows that the energy is with us, the zeitgeist is with us, and of course with our authors. I can't take all the credit.

Blackwell:* So since that's where you are now, where do you see it going in—

Hovgaard: The origin of it was very simple. The best ideas are always very simple. I saw this statistic, I can't quote it for you off the top of my head, but something like X percent, 80% or something like that, of fiction was being purchased by womxn. And I thought, right away, the market is distorted. Do men not have money? Men can read, right? It was practically a godsend, this idea that there's a market sitting there, waiting, they have money, they're saying, give us something to consume.

Blackwell: **And from that, you developed the concept of WILF.**

Hovgaard: Yes. *Writers I'd Like to Follow*. What business comes down to, what entrepreneurship comes down to, is basically one thing: the idea. You look at social media, you look where people are, and you say, make this convertible.

Blackwell: **Describe it, for anyone unfamiliar with your offerings.**

Hovgaard: First and foremost, it's about empowering womxn. But it is a form of empowerment which acknowledges and understands that we need to convert to sales with a male consumer base. Which in my view is the ultimate form of empowerment for womxn. Because it shows them where their opportunities lie, where they belong, where men need them to be. And we are very sex-positive, very anti-patriarchal. We are smashing that stuff. There's that expression, shake your moneymaker. To me, that's girl power. The epiphany for me was the understanding that you put the author out front. We're not just telling stories, we are selling authors. The trampoline video was really the one which we saw driving engagement.

Blackwell: **You're referring to a viral video series in which your authors gave readings of their work while bouncing on a trampoline. In what might be called dampened attire.**

Hovgaard: Wet T-shirts. We can call it what it is, with the caveat that this is all done in the spirit of sex-positivity. There was a lot of slut-shaming out there, directed at our authors and at our press. We welcome it. It's engagement, and engagement drives the algo. The answer is to get excited about this stuff. We want to excite our readers, we are aiming for excitement, we ourselves are always excited, constant excitement, to the point that it's an itch you feel like you will never be able to scratch, it builds and builds, until you achieve release, which, immediately before that point, we are aiming to convert to a sale.

Blackwell: **Your press's strategies for driving sales are proverbial for their inventiveness.**

Hovgaard: The best ideas are the simplest ideas, like I said. Everyone loves a ranking, and so, what do you do? You rank your authors. People love the Oscars, they love awards, they want to see their favorite writer crowned, recognized—it is like you yourself are being recognized, you identify with the writer, their success is yours.

We started doing this from the first issue of our fiction anthology, *WILF69*. You had 69 authors, all womxn, of course, and the sort of authors who really fit our brand, our look, there was just this incredible energy. Young, full of artistic drive, a variety of body types and skin tones. And then we left it to the fans, to the readers. You buy a copy of the anthology, it includes an official ballot. You use the ballot to vote for your favorite writer. The guys have very strong opinions about these things, you see it in the comments section on the trampoline videos, they are very sure about who they want to be at the top of the pyramid. Like, a human pyramid of girl writers. So they cast their ballots, and that's how we determine who the top author is in each monthly contest. She rises in the rankings like that one bird, from the ashes.

Blackwell: **The phoenix. So, one key facet is that readers can cast multiple ballots.**

Hovgaard: There is one ballot in each copy of the anthology. If you want to vote 20 times, you buy 20 anthologies. I believe in allowing the market to decide. That's the purest outcome. If someone is dedicated, they buy more of the product. Everything is interchangeable: dedication, passion, true feeling right from the heart—and money, capital—and books, content, product. Our authors are incredibly engaging, they look great, they are the girl next door, they are the Venus in Furs, they are the goddess you cannot reach, but this is your chance. You can support her, you can help her, you will be her patron, you will be her daddy. So they vote. Pure economic democracy.

Let me tell you something. This just blows my mind, it is awesome, and I don't use that word lightly—it is *awesome.* We heard of guys, probably middle-aged, living at home still, disposable income, these literature fans were bulk-buying hundreds of copies of the anthology, boxes of books, and they were even hiring college kids to work part-time to open up these anthologies for them, I mean open up the shrink-wrap, pull out the ballot, and fill it in to vote for the guy's favorite author. I just love that shit, it's so entrepreneurial in spirit, I feel this sense of, you know, like being a kindred spirit. These guys were dedicated, they really wanted their favorite author to win.

I take pride in the idea that we hit the top of every chart, every ranking, and probably, I'll go out on a limb and say, maybe 5% of the physical books that we sold ended up being read. A lot of them went right in the bin, you extract the ballot and you've got what you paid for, what do you need the actual book for? Some people say that's somehow a problem. To me, it's inspiring. It demonstrates the level of dedication. Nobody else has ever done this in literature or publishing. We are blazing the trail here.

***Blackwell:* And the rest is history.**

Hovgaard: That doesn't mean anything. History doesn't even exist. Now that we've done this, anybody else could do it too. It's a free market, everyone is free to do anything, it's frankly terrifying. We have to come up with the next thing, the next wave of leveraging our authors, and it's terrifying. Thankfully the destructive power of technology is opening up new pathways to growth, new creative pathways. We have AI now. I mean, we're talking trampolines to the nth power.

***Blackwell:* So, is the future AI-generated novels?**

Hovgaard: That's a stupid question. Again, you're thinking in the old paradigm. The future is the AI-generated novelist. That's what artists and creators in our time are having a hard time readjusting to, but it's coming, and if you want to earn money out there, what are you going to do? The answer is to get excited about it.

So of course the novel itself is AI-generated, but also you need an author's persona, you need the headshot, you need the bio, you need the social media presence, engaging with consumers, BookTok videos, fan-service photo shoots, there's all these moving parts. *AI can generate all that for you*, and then you're producing content at scale.

The exciting thing about AI is that it replaces something imperfect, it perfects it—we're not there yet, but if you have a little bit of vision you can see this coming—and the Writers I'd Like to Follow are going to be superseded by writers that you practically have no choice but to follow, writers who are constructed for you, constructed in a sense by you because they are constructed from a close AI analysis of your media consumption patterns.

Blackwell: **Critics of that kind of thing say that it will lack a human element, but—**

Hovgaard: Wrong, wrong, wrong. The AI is human. We can say that very definitively. It's human because it is trained on humanity. We teach it to be human. And it's the best sort of human because it is very productive. That's what we need as a society, right? We need someone to produce so that we can consume.

Right now there is this incredible burden that's placed on the consumer, which is that, in the act of consuming something, you have to support someone else's lifestyle. I liken it to a protection racket. You know, there's a neighborhood where the mob runs everything, you go to the laundromat and you're paying money to have your clothing cleaned, but a significant chunk of that money has to go to support the local mob, who are threatening to burn down the laundromat if they don't pay the protection money. It's parasitic. And that's how a lot of the economy works. You just want to consume, you don't necessarily want to send some author's kids to college. The consumer shouldn't be responsible for paying for some author's kid's orthodontic bill. So the amount of money, which in the first place to be honest is not that huge, but that money being paid to the creators of what we consume, it's a burden; the public should not be on the hook for that.

So you have technology, it comes in, it disrupts. The AI, the beautiful thing is, it's not parasitic. It produces efficiently, it produces exactly what we need, it gives us the chance to consume efficiently and economically.

Blackwell: **But what does this mean for the authors in your stable?**

Hovgaard: We are committed to them. We do everything we can for them. It's like a family.

Blackwell: **So when they are replaced by AI...?**

Hovgaard: Certain things just can't be avoided. Authors write because they have a dream, a passionate drive, and that in itself is the true reward. But we're dedicated to them and we appreciate them and they are really the lifeblood and, you know, what else can I say? They are artists, and art is a service, and the pleasure of the servant is in pleasing the master. That's what it boils down to. That's art. It's a fantastic opportunity.

***

ABOUT THE INTERVIEWER: R. Woebeset Blackwell has won the Guggenheim, the Tendt Prize in long-form fiction, the Iowa Poetry Prize, an NEH transliteration grant, the Grey Seal Nonfiction Prize, a Knight-Bietz Foundation mixed media prize, the O. Henry Award for the short story, and a Pushcart Prize for the pseudofictional essay. Four-time winner of the Massachusetts Foundation for the Arts fellowship, she has also been awarded Meadlands, Fromitage, James Merrill, Yaddo, McDonnell, and Ferrero residencies. She has a short story collection (La Puerta Falsa Books) and a poetry chapbook (BeBold Press) forthcoming, and lives in Manhattan with her partner, a hedge-fund manager.

LoveReads aka Niomi S_________, Number Three Ranked Reader Reels in the Big Fish

Ryszard Merey

A timorous vibration on her screen. A tentative tiny flame. Feed me. Make me bigger. Niomi cracked her knuckles and settled her fingers back over the keyboard. Her nails were distressedly short, all but the pinky on her left hand, curving a conspicuous half-inch off of her finger and painted a venomous green. It was the only nail with any color. The rest were lacquerless, chipped. They flickered over keys while, just beyond her peripherals, Beef wandered dazily in the refuse on her desk.

–You really think so?

The unanswered question beat on her screen, fragile and needy as a preemie mouse. Niomi applied the eyedropper of warm milk deftly.

–Yes. That's why I had to write you. I'm glad to see you're up too. I was sure you'd be asleep by now and wouldn't see this message until much later.

Liar liar. Niomi knew it wasn't night time in Rosaro's part of the world, and that he most likely had been doing everything but sleeping, hunched breathlessly on the other side of the screen. Waiting for this exact message. She didn't know it, but she knew it. That's the kind of Writer he was. She'd been up the whole night too, having planned and succeeded in finishing *Dyception: Rumble in the UAE,* at precisely this hour—her 5:30 a.m. Obviously, she could have stopped reading at any time before. Laid her head down like a normalo and written him in her morning, after a night of rest. But she genuinely believed it was that touch of authenticity that gave her the edge on the other Readers.

You don't rise to Number Three by phoning it in.

This is what Frey had never managed to comprehend. Pay attention to those little tells; customize your Writ's experience to reel them in. Got it? Of course, Nio. I'm not a bloody idiot, they'd snapped. Being proud and needing to be Great at Everything was vintage Frey. But this just wasn't their field. Poor thing, never breaking into the Top Fifty, hadn't managed to ken Beelzebub's address. But Niomi knew exactly where to find Old Screwtape, apartment floor and unit number and all. The Devil, she knew, lived right in the—

A crucial detail she had not missed: for all he said, Rosaro ached for her to stay up half the night reading. It was his deepest desire. He wanted it more than he wanted his fat year-end bonus. He wanted it more than he wanted the sex-ice between him and his wife to thaw. His heart yearned most to experience, at least once in his life, the exquisite thrill of a Reader getting labyrinthed in his story. A reader losing sleep because they were JUST THAT IN-VESTED in a situation born entirely out of his head. So I really hope this doesn't wake you up, but it's 5:30 in the morning, and I'm writing to tell you that I was up until now. I just had to know the ending.

Rosaro Johansson. Listed in his profile as originally from the US. Currently living in Madrid. CFO of a software development firm. Previous work in military intelligence. *Dyception* is his first novel. A superspy working in a highly classified project is hired to track one of the most dangerous men in Europe, kicking off a risiko-laden cat and mouse crescendoing to a final bloody showdown in the UAE. Dashes of Interpol. Hefty sprankles of chiseled self-insert pining for his emotionally constipated Anglopretty assistant, Dr. Kendoll. Homoerotic tension simmering like a torrid hundred-hour ragu, until the last chapter, where the writer threw every switch to eleven. Great plot, hot sex, holyshitballswhatthefuckisthisshit writing, Rosaro. If that was even his real name. But sure, the storyteller persona was half the glamour. Rosaro could've been an expat in Madrid, drowning his clichéd midlife woes in a cool sea of glyphs. A younger man, donning an elite corpo mask to inject 'authenticity' into the story. An old man, rewriting his military desk-past with more jetskis! More breasts! More Interpol! A woman who didn't think any Reader would give a female espionage writer a fair shake. Rosaro could've been absolutely anyone.

But Niomi played along. After all, she had personas too: meek Mia, a soft-typing twenty-two-year-old communications student who had wanted to become a writer more than anything. More than ANYTHING (controlling parents and a submissive personality throttled that). A Writer who wanted deep, emotional, but ultimately positive engagement went well with Mia. Then there was Crimson, a cranky thirtysomething anachrodyke cum social worker, combing the interwebs ruthlessly for the Next Great Read to amnesia the fact that she herself couldn't cut it. Couldn't write anything good enough to Platinum. Gallbladder bitter. If a Writer wanted to phoenix a project from the spattered brain batter of their curbstomped first draft, Crimson was just the Reader. Frail, Healthy, even Strong Egos need not apply.

In this very moment though, Niomi was Toby. One of her older personas. Forty-eight years old. Homemaker husband and diligent feedbackist. Financially and time-privileged, stuck in a frosty marriage that eerily mirrored Rosaro's (except, unlike Rosaro, he didn't play the hetero). Toby wasn't a writer himself, but he read relentlessly. Hundreds of thousands of words a week.

Fastidious, demure Toby. Whose own creative ambitions had long ago atrophied back into a harmless, desiccated claw. True crime and espionage fiction with Kleenex-thin self-inserts were his absolute favorite. Niomi had accepted Rosaro's work ticket about three days ago, and based on his profile and their short meet-and-greet text-chat, had found herself slipping into Toby's voice almost immediately. Every project needed a different type of Reader and *Dyception: Rumble in the UAE* desperately needed Toby—a version of him she customized to fit the dimensions of this exact project. Niomi-Toby typed:

–I don't say this to everyone, but—
–Yes?

She allowed an appropriately gravitased pause before letting her stained fingertips hit the keys again. Just outside her range of vision, the shitty unit around her sighed and reeled. Blades of light started to slash through the pull-downs—Niomi kept her single window covered day and night. Often, the blades of light creeping, then slowly sweeping over different parts of the room—her dingy mattress, her one chair with clothes, her floor trashed with trash—were her only observable metric of passing time.

Other than the ludicrously large clock pulsing perpetually on her LoveReads App.

You have _ _ hours and _ _ minutes to finish this project and submit your feedback.

She typed to Rosaro now. Looked at the sentence shimmering on the sickly screen to confirm no typos (Niomi made typos, but Toby did not), then hit send.

–I really think you should submit this. I really think this story could go... Platinum.

A wasted carrot on anybody under forty; people with their head above ground knew that Platinum badges and the eponymous publishing house itself was a hollow joke. Another trap to dupe the Dupes. The great Creative Bubble had burst before she was born, but the older blokes still liked to mime the Before Times, and Niomi had a hunch that Rosaro was older. Maybe as old as her own father. Still, though, you can get backstabbed by a hunch. She squirmed but finally, the screen flashed back his response—

–You can't seriously... Come on. Blush symbol. Blush symbol.

A sigh of relief. Gentlemen. We're in.

–I do mean it. That finale! And that subtle nod to Ian Flemming—it was so classy, and I just don't... Damn it, I don't see writing like this anymore. I think you could go somewhere with this. I don't say that lightly, or to everyone.

Toby really didn't.

Oh, that flock of fools who thought all it took to be a Love Reader was barfing compliments over anyone you read. Wait, you mean, I get paid to sit in my bedroom, read all day in my sharty underwear and BS to writers about how Platinum their writing is?? Sign me up!!!

No, they did not get it. Two eyes open and a mouthole drooling platitudes weren't enough. You needed ALL eyes open to catch that shimmer, more subtle than the scintillation on a hummingbird's wing. The minutest angle, and the color was different. Or gone. So many DIDN'T want adulation. Their self-loathing would have rendered it instantly unusable as feedback. Repulsive. They craved complex, structured confusion; critical, intricate engagement—hell, some wanted a new set of orifices, or a bashed-in heart or skull. A punch in the metaphorical mouth and a couple of missing teeth. Most treacherous was that a frightening amount said they wanted one thing, while hopelessly craving another. Your eyes ears pores, even your shithole had to be harvesting and titrating emotions constantly to keep your bread butterside UP.

Readers who tried to mindlessly asslick their way through the job would never break past the hundredth Rank. Back when they still lived together, even Frey, who had been relatively astute and worked just as tirelessly as her, had peaked and plateaued hard at the 164th Rank. Oh how it had killed them to watch Niomi climb higher and higher while they stayed stalled. But Niomi had what it took, yes. Which was why if she clicked over to the LoveReads Dashboard << Ranking << Top Earners on the site, her avi (a tiny, tasteful black-and-white ink sketch of a rat) kept its tenacious hover in the third spot. *(Every seven seconds a Reader is falling in Love with a new Book! Why not yours? Find YOUR dream Reader today! Every month, the Readers' Favorite Story is recommended to Platinum—the one and ONLY Platinum Publishing LightHouse in a sea of Unread, Forgettable Content. So why not YOUR Book? Connect with your Writing Dream Today!)* Sometimes, she herself could not believe it. The Third-highest earner. The Third-best provider of a customizable, personal audience. And if she kept this up, she would be the Second. Or even the First Love Reader. *(Every month, we give out credit prizes to our top earning Love Readers, who keep the most Writers satisfied and eager to turn in more Content to be Love Read! It's a Virtuous Circle! So why not You? Become a Precious Writer's Dream Reader today! More for us, more for You—most for our Precious Writers!)*

But the whales were still out there. Somewhere. Niomi would have traded her Third status (or even the Second or the First rank, had she possessed either), and her left gray eye and her right pinky toe and a piece of her kidney, and a good three millimeters of her sphincter for a Luxury Reader gig: get yourself an entire furnished unit from one of those gaga rich patrons shitting out three books a month (all of them using artificial assistance).

Sure, the writing suffered—on LoveReads, the chance of reading a good story wasn't drastically less likely than reading a terrible one, whereas Luxury Readers spent their entire reading lives inhaling football fields of robot-generated pap. But the credits were out of this galaxy, and these captive audiences of one lived the charmed lives of manicured little storyforcefed geese. For a glyph-jockey like Niomi, that didn't sound half bad. She loved the solitary peace of reading, always had—crime fiction or gothic horror or Jacobean revenge plays or babysitter paranormal fantasy—plus, real black tea every morning, and a little rhinestone leash for Beef! Set for life, but...

Niomi wasn't there. Not yet. Currently, a contracted Reader. Paying for her own capsule, her own food, and her own supply of Night Beats with the credits she earned on LoveReads. But still, the third-most-contracted Reader, on the number one love-reading site on the interwebs, and THAT was nothing to sneeze at.

ACHOO!

To the right, Beef scurried over her scar-latticed arm, then sat on his hind legs, twitching his whiskers in the gloom. She puckered a kiss in his direction. "I know, baby. It's dusty in here. Let me just finish this chat with Rosaro and then maybe we can take a little walk. We're almost out of your treats."

Beef's favorite snack was dried apricots, and there was indeed only one left on the little baggie amongst the other rubbish on her desk. Her pet rat might have been the only reason Niomi ever stuck her own snout out these days—came with the job—the constant dips of Night Beats to keep you awake torpedoed the appetite. Niomi had been reading for 47 hours straight now—she hadn't slept in three days, hadn't eaten in two, hadn't showered in six and hadn't shat in five. But that's what it took. And you never knew.

Rosaro was a new user and maybe he'd be the one to make her his One Reader, and set her up in a fancy unit, with a new rig, and all the dried apricots Beef could stuff into his adorable white ratty cheeks. Not to mention... She took a swig of tepid water from a lidded cup on her desk and turned back to the screen again. Beef nibbled on the last apricot, then started to fidget through her cemetery of mugs. Niomi's desktop was an open mass grave of abandoned drinks, mold specimens and nutrient-bar wrappers. Focus, Nio. It was now six in the morning and she willed her blurry eyes to sharpen on the screen and let her tie up her chat with Rosaro.

On his submission form, he'd said that he wanted brutal honesty, but Niomi's wide-open pores whispered to her—go down that road, and he will never write another word again. Reeling in the fish was such a delicate enterprise: aspartametalk the wrong Writer, and they'll pay out their month fee, no tip, and never contract you again. Their exit review will tank your ranking and advertise to the whole site your perceived arrogance. I said I wanted honesty! You think I don't know that my writing is shit? You're not even a real Reader. Worthless asskisser! @community, do not contract this person; your senile gramma will give you the same rah rah drivel and for free!

Rosaro however, was not that guy. He said he wanted Honesty, but he didn't know what he wanted. Good thing a pro in the top Three knew: Rosaro wanted his Writing Kissed, Licked and Worshiped. Deepthroat the shaft and guzzle the gravy.

Niomi's hands settled back over the keys. She wouldn't doubt her hunch again.

–When you gave that nod to Flemming in the very last showdown... Did I tell you that my late father had every Ian Flemming novel and I binge-read those over and over as a kid? And then, when the Sheik came in to... Jesus. I just wish my dad was still around. He would enjoy this book so much.

–Oh... I can't believe you caught that detail, with the Sheik.– Rosaro's enthusiasm coursed through the screen.

–I've never had anyone catch that! God, what am I saying? I've never had anyone read this, so of course nobody had caught it. But I never thought anyone would, even if they DID read it! I tried to get my wife to give it a go last year, but...

They type-chatted and, word by word, the shaved-head wraith in a stinking capsule unit, bent over the azure back-lit keys with a pet rat scurrying up her scarred-up arm metamorphed: fresh, pristine air, mug of real brewed coffee, marquis skin, strawberry curls, suburban kitchen, razorthin laptop, kitchen island, luxurious Italian marble, perfection. Elegant. Earnest. Not so erudite. But so, so enthusiastic. Toby typed, breathlessly:

–I know you must be rather busy with your regular job and I really don't mean to pry or push you out of your comfort zone, but would it be possible to read something else from you?

A tick and Niomi shivered. A skinslice of doubt—idiot—don't remind him of that—but then there it came. Almost immediate. An orgasmic wave of gratitude washed through the screen, so rich and potent, it tsunamied her body straight from two continents over.

–I... oh my god. I... I don't even know what to say, Toby. Are you sure?

Be so good, they forget it's transactional. She typed back.

–Absolutely. It was a pleasure to read your story, and I can't wait to read more from you.

–I... I'm just so... Hearing that makes my entire week. No, my whole month.

–Well, I haven't enjoyed a book this much in a very long time, so I'm really happy to hear that. Anyway, apologies, but I must go to bed now. My husband is leaving for another summit this morning, and he will expect me to be up to see him off.

–And you've been up all night. Reading my silly book.

–Nothing I would have rather spent the night doing. I was on the edge of my seat.

–Blush symbol. Is your husband gone often?

–Yes. That's why I have so much time to read. Silver lining. Good night, Rosaro.

–Good night, Toby. Thank you again. Let's talk soon.

Niomi shook her cramping fingers out. Remembered, and dutifully set the LoveReads status on her Rosaro-facing account to 'sleeping.' But in other parts of the world, her account status listed her as awake—

Ding.

```
New! You have a new LoveReads re-
quest!
Username: Coldfyre1
Author name: Willa Coldfyre
Genre: Sapphic revenant erotica (ex-
plicit)
Working title: LoveBytes
Molly is a software engineer. Camil-
la is an occult scientist. They're
about to tie the knot, when happily
ever after goes horrifically wrong.
Both left for dead, only one wakes up.
And then it's back to the lab with her
fiance's corpse—until Cami realizes
that she's dead too. Too bad for them,
they didn't kill her memories when
```

they killed her body. A completely
bonkers and brutally ruthless sapphic revenge-spatter horror.
  Warnings: lesbophobia, fatphobia,
necrophilia, coprophilia, cannibal-
ism, torture, rape, abuse, murder.
  Word count: 350,000 words
  Chat feedback: Up to 10,000 words
  Deadline: 48 hours
  Author note: Listen, I know I'm
paying you for this, so let's cut
the shit. No BS and no smoke blown
up my ass. Just read my book and tell
me what you think. If you're not at
least an 80 Ranked Reader, get bent.
Cheers, dumbfucks— Willa.

  Congratulations, N30N30! You are
Writer Coldfyre1's FIRST CHOICE for
this LoveReads project! You have
(ticker counting down) minutes to
officially become The Reader for
this book, before the offer is
opened to all ranked Readers. Do you
Accept or Reject?

Niomi tapped a finger in the corner of her herpe'd
mouth. The book enticed for sure, but what about
Rosaro? This could take a lot of energy and, while their

chat had ended on a bright note, she hadn't yet gotten any sign of a—

Ding.

From the other side of her desk, she grabbed her ancient phone and flipped it open. Her rig was already flashing the notif on her LoveReads account, but she chose to read it off her phone's app instead.

```
A LoveReads notification.
Writer Rosaro554 has sent you a gift
of 500 credits.
Note: I wish this was more. You
deserve so much more, Toby. Thank
you. I cannot tell you how much your
feedback meant to me, but I hope this
gives you an idea. I'm all fired up
and ready to write tomorrow. Flaming
heart symbol. Heart shot with an arrow
symbol. Infinity symbol. Book symbol.
```

Five hundred. The phone fell from her hand to the grody floor while Niomi leaned back in her chair. Wet warmth spread from between her legs, up her body, and, behind closed eyes, for the first time in a long time, she saw Frey's handsome andro face sharpened in anger. That day they'd finally packed it up and jumped for good. Yeah, fuck this, Nio. I'm out. You said you wanted to have something together, but all you care about is reading... and fucking... credits... and that dumb... RAT. That's it. That's all life will ever be to you. Just stay the fuck away from people, okay? You don't have room for me. You don't have room for anyone.

Niomi let herself lay in her chair for 49 seconds, credit glow cascading through her torso, arms, fingers, eartips, and clit. Then she picked up her phone. Tipped out an appropriately ecstatic (but not gauche and not too sloppy) thank you to Rosaro, then flicked to her LoveReads dashboard and hit 'accept' on Willa's book. As the Third Ranked Reader, bombarded by read requests constantly and roosting at the very top of ten thousand Love Writers' waiting lists, she had more or less the literary pick of the litter. This accept would be the highlight of this foul-mouth Willa's whole damn year. LoveBytes was a fuck-awful name, but Niomi just knew that the prose would be amazing, and that the characters and tension would nail her to her seat, and once in a while, to treat herself, she liked to pick a book that could actually warrant Platinum accolades. Even better, she could smell from Willa's three personal lines a prideful hyena who couldn't stoop to acknowledge even a smidgen of kindness (earned or not). Who just wanted to be knocked to the ground and squatted over, her book torn up and spit out and sprinkled mockingly back over her nutrientbar-runny-shit-spattered body. A humiliation to then gleefully harness to flagellate herself into a frenzied production of an even more massive, even more spectacularly fucked-up cult-cunt-tingler of a horror epic. Again, and again, and aga… As long as nobody ever truly acknowledged her raw talent, that fuck-these-peasants energy could be creatively milked indefinitely. That's what Willa needed from her. And Niomi could give it.

But not without a little help.

She rummaged on her desk; gripped her pot of Night Beats. Damn, she was running low on that too. Either she'd have to call in Eddy to bring a delivery, or really venture out later tonight, carting li'l Beef in her oversized coat's pocket. But that was for later. Taking the tiny pot, Niomi screwed the top off carefully, then dipped four millimeters of her long pinkie-nail's trough into the neon purple powder. Deposited it deftly into her left nostril. Sniffed just hard enough to make the powder stick, thinking, this was the last book, really. After this, she'd take a break. No Night Beats for at least a week.

And a shower. And a real night in bed. And a real plate of food, before her digestive tract completely conked out. And maybe even an Open the Window? And how about a Take Out The Festering Trash? But first—

Niomi turned back to her glowing screen. Clicked the file open. Here was Molly and Camilla. Gorgeously, foreverly in love. Perfect jobs. Bright and spanking futures. On their way to get married. But then, their car breaks down...

Dirtypuddle eyes refracted the glare of the screen. Beef scurried to his water dispenser, set up in an open cage on the end of the desk, then curled into an abandoned beanie he sometimes used as his nest. Niomi's phone got a new notification, and right on its heels, another one, but she'd put it on manner mode, and her device sat untouched on the edge of her desk. Nothing would disturb this project for Willa. For the next eight hours, Niomi wouldn't be doing anything but reading, stopping very rarely to take a sip of water, and even more rarely, to pee in a bottle she kept right under her desk. Dedication and speed were what kept her at Ranking Number Three.

So the messages throbbed patiently in her phone. Unread.

New Notification
From your LoveReads Team
Writer Rosaro554 has sent you a gift of 500 credits.
Damn it all, my wife is going to have a fit at the end of the month, but you're so worth it, Toby. God, I'm still thinking about what you said. Finding you on this site was the best thing that ever happened to me. Hope you're sleeping well. Book symbol. Night symbol. Pistol symbol. Salute symbol.

New Notification
From: M_____
Nio, I talked to Dr. Simbal, they said they're going to have to operate on Lili as soon as possible. Thank you for sending those 1000 credits last week. That will be enough to bribe the nurses and make sure she gets the proper food. We're going in this morning, and I know you are probably reading right now and won't see this for at least a half day… Kina said she'll come over this next week, to help out. Anyway, just wanted to give

you an update. Don't work too hard, angel.

Mama would be so lost without you two.

THE LAST AUTHOR

Rohan O'Duill

Brondan watched from the swivel armchair, face to face with @dragonslayer2089, whose scrawny body and gaunt features would seem to dispute the validity of his username. Dragon Slayer typed the 101-character long Bleet into the holo keyboard before triumphantly tapping SEND. The live audience craned their necks to watch the Bleet scroll across the big screen.

Are you even able to start your morning without a coffee? I need two shots before I can see straight.

Brondan squinted out into the darkness of the jam-packed auditorium to gauge the reaction to Dragon Slayer's Bleet. The movement was minimal and the cheers muted.

None of these people understood what Flippit meant to Brondan. Some contestants were here to win, most just wanted their moment in the sun, but for Brondan this was retribution.

Spinning the chair back to the big screen behind them, they watched the numbers flying up on the readout. Dragon Slayer whizzed away on his keyboard, replying to as many comments as possible to keep that algo moving. But Brondan wasn't worried. That Bleet was tired, and everyone knew it. There was no way something so pedestrian was going to knock them off their pedestal.

The three-minute timer buzzed an ending to the Bleet run, and Brondan's opponent had clicked up 3.7 million interactions. Not bad, but nothing on Brondan's 5.2 million score. This match was going to be a breeze.

Brondan cracked their knuckles and stretched their neck from side to side, bad habits from too much time spent hunched over a keyboard. But the familiar actions sent a welcome tingle of dogged determination through their body. Next was the pun round. This is what Brondan had been born for. Their fingers reached out into the neon green of the holo and tapped away at the characters.

The other day a book fell on my head, I guess I only have my shelf to blame.

The auditorium erupted with laughter and Brondan's interaction levels went wild.

Brondan had been saving this Bleet for years. It was the ultimate author pun. And now they had pulled it out at exactly the right time. There was no way they could be caught now. They were through the first round.

***

Brondan warmed up in the swarming backstage area, careful not to strike any of the passing crew with stretching arms. They had worked with a choreographer on a number of routines for the past two years for this round. But the song they had chosen was a new release to keep the algo happy, so the routine wasn't as imprinted in their brain as it had been with previous songs.

Brondan was ushered onto the stage, now transformed with raised platforms and dazzling lights. It was one thing to watch this theatre from a screen at home, but being here under the heat of the lights and the stare of a thousand eyes, Brondan felt like an ant. The music started, and the bassy night beats gave Brondan the confidence to start moving. The TicCok round was on.

They threw their arms in the air, twirled and popped their hips forward, calves and groin muscles twitching as they kicked perilously high above their head. The song climaxed and so did the audience as Brondan jumped and landed in a half-splits at the crescendo. The applause seemed to last forever. The likes flowed in like heroin injected straight into their veins. The numbers on the big screen spiralled out of control. This could be one of the biggest scores ever in the Pit.

There was no doubt Brondan had made it into the third and final round.

***

Next up was the stunt round. And Brondan had spent far more time choreographing this stunt than the dance routine.

The stage hands rolled on the massive Wheel of Death, ten metres of shiny chrome track that looped up and around, just like Brondan's childhood Skidmarks car set. But this loop-the-loop was no toy: flames spouted randomly, hungry for a victim.

The mechanic handed Brondan the electric kick scooter. "Good luck. The last fella broke his back on that thing, and it wasn't tweaked like this one," the mechanic said with a glint in their eye.

It had been so easy to convince the mechanic to replace the normal battery with what Brondan had told him was a souped-up version. A couple of hundred credits and the mechanic had believed Brondan's scheme was just to help them win the competition.

"The YouBoob stage is a killer," Brondan replied with a wink.

Brondan walked out in front of the audience and slowly began to open the buttons on their pink sequined top. The crowd giggled in anticipation. Lots of performers disrobed during stunts to help with the algo. But Brondan had other plans.

The open shirt revealed a printed T-shirt with the simple message: COMPLY OR DIE. Brondan pulled the battery pack from the scooter and, with a click, removed the casing, revealing the green bubbling liquid inside the vial. They held up the lethal device, pressing down on the dead man's switch.

"I have just armed this weapon to distribute VX nerve agent throughout this building if I release the pressure on my thumb. If anybody moves or tries anything at all, everyone in this room will perish."

Panicked chatter rolled through the gathered crowd as the audience tittered back and forth on whether this was part of the stunt or not. But the emergency protocol locked down the studio—which it would only do in response to biological weapons. The AI security system wouldn't risk releasing it into the outside world. The lawsuits would cost far too much money, while everyone inside signed away their rights as soon as they pressed purchase on the tickets.

Brondan looked over their shoulder. Their numbers were taking off like a rocket.

"I want to see Mr. Book. Now." Brondan's voice quavered.

"I am here," a voice boomed through the speakers as Mr. Book's face appeared on the big screen. There had been no time for make-up or skin-tape. Mr. Book's jowls danced below his chin, and those little beady eyes peered out above puffy red-veined cheeks. All the while, the viewership figures spun out of control at the corner of the screen.

Brondan had had no idea it would be this easy to speak to the man himself. Nao Hovgaard was *the* legend of modern publishing. At first everyone had called him an innovator when he made UpWomxn Books a success in a struggling industry. Then they called him a shrewd businessman as he managed to take over the last of the big publishing houses. And then by moving them each into different jurisdictions he was able to merge them into a single company: The Big One. Once he owned every company, he made the transition to fully AI-generated books, laying off hundreds of thousands of staff in the process. Everyone else had struggled to generate human-sounding books with AI. But Hovgaard figured it out. The key had been separate AI systems. Creative AI to generate the first draft, a second developmental AI, followed by a third editorial AI. All were completely singular entities. Together they created the perfect books for consumers. At first the term Mr. Book was a slur thrown at Hovgaard for destroying a whole industry. But Hovgaard had embraced the name and gone by Book ever since.

To appease the anti-AI lobby that consisted predominantly of ex-authors and artists, Mr. Book had also created FlipPit. An event to pick one human author to be published every year. Brondan had spent eight years practising for this year's FlipPit event. And now it was time to make Book pay.

"I want you to delete the creator AI, or everyone in this building dies," Brondan demanded.

After the cries of outrage and dismay faded in the auditorium, Mr. Book laughed. "And let unreliable and tardy authors back into the job? You have no idea how hard it was working with human authors. They just don't do what they are told."

"You will have the death of thousands of people on your hands if you don't do it," Brondan said, sounding less and less sure of themself as the sweat dripped from their forehead and the murderous vial gained weight by the second. Could they really set off the device if Mr. Book refused their demand?

Brondan caught sight of the television feed on a screen behind the stage. Their tiny silhouette below the gigantic slovenly face of Mr. Book. The David and Goliath image gave them strength as they lifted the vial threateningly towards the camera.

"I have a counteroffer for you," Mr. Book replied, a sly smile revealing perfect teeth between the botoxed sausage-lips. "You have proved here tonight that you have the creativity and tenacity to be a truly brilliant author. Your viewership numbers have smashed every record possible. I am willing to offer you a deal. Not one book this year. No, one book every year for the rest of your life. You will be the most famous human author this century."

The AI had taken Brondan's parents' jobs. It had left them destitute. Growing up in homeless hostels, living off food stamps. Brondan had been so sure of their cause all this time. Yet here and now, their mind muddled. They found they were considering the offer.

Presumably seeing the hesitation, Mr. Book poured honey on the deal. "Imagine the WickedPedia page: Dickens, Fitzgerald, Sanderson and now Brondan Lowring. I am having the contract made up as we speak."

"But I haven't written a single chapter, never mind a book," Brondan squeaked out, to a mixture of gasps and laughter from the audience. "Like, I have been meaning to. I have lots of outlines. I just haven't found the time to get to the draft."

"We have seen your Bleets and have every confidence that with our support you will create books that will sell millions. Plus, with both yours and the FlipPit winners' books being released every year, you will still reduce the number of AI-authored books in the market. You will succeed in your goal."

Could this offer be real? Could Brondan be the 22nd century's Dickens? Just as their mom had dreamt of being. People needed real-life authors. Just like their dad had aspired to become. Brondan had a responsibility to the world, to humanity. Brondan could tell their story, paint AI in its true form. Educate the planet. Brondan would be the greatest author ever.

Murmurings from the audience developed into a chant: "TAKE THE DEAL, TAKE THE DEAL."

Brondan swallowed hard. "Where do I sign?"

ALICIA'S REVISION

Tucker Lieberman

It was 1924 already, and the novelist had feverish writer's block. His publisher was demanding to know where his book was. He'd promised to have it ready by the new year, but on the second day of February he still didn't even have a first chapter. Ruminating on his approaching 36th birthday, he lamented his underperformance.

Then someone called him to offer a deal.

On foot, he passed Bogotá's police headquarters, which had gone up the previous year, and the Liévano palace for city business, only several years older, designed and rebuilt after a fire destroyed the earlier building, which had in turn replaced what an earthquake had destroyed. There was always a second chance, or so he hoped.

He turned into La Puerta Falsa, a hundred-year-old restaurant recommended by Señorita Rolo. She hadn't arrived. He ordered a hot chocolate. As he broke up the side of cheese into small pieces and dropped it into the mug, he saw her walk into the room. She sat across from him and ordered a tamal santafereño.

"As I told you," she said, after pleasantries, "I have a solution—if you can pay for it." She unwrapped the banana leaf from the warm tamal.

"I'm ready."

"I have a manuscript," she said, toying with her fork.

He snorted. "I can't publish your manuscript."

"It's not my manuscript. I didn't write it. Arturo Cova did."

"Oh?"

Señorita Rolo smiled. Of course, that made a difference to him—that a man wrote it.

Now he was willing to listen. "Who's Arturo Cova?" he asked.

"A young womanizer in Bogotá," she said matter-of-factly. "The law came after him for taking advantage of a young unmarried woman, and his girlfriend's parents kicked her out of the house. Alicia was a city girl who had never ridden a horse, yet somehow they fled east on horseback, into the Amazon, to Casanare, letting the campfire smolder all night by their hammocks to scare away big cats. Out there in the elements—ducks, parrots, egrets, macaws, the rising sun—imagine it! They weren't really in love with each other," she added. "But Alicia was pregnant. Cova felt he owed her something, but he couldn't really see the situation from her perspective. Ultimately he could only tell his own story. His imagination encompassed only himself. He wrote everything down, every contradictory passing thought, before he died. He never made it out of the jungle, but we still have his words."

"He must have made enemies. Wouldn't they recognize his story? How could I publish it under my name?"

"He had enemies, perhaps, but they're all dead. Narciso Barrera was one. Barrera's business was recruiting desperate people to extract rubber from trees, and he'd made a lot of money off their labor. Cova and Alicia were staying at a cattle ranch in Casanare when this fellow showed up to find more workers. He took an interest in Alicia, or Alicia took an interest in him—anyway, the two of them split from Cova. Cova followed them, wanting to kill Barrera and recover Alicia, though—I should say again—he wasn't in love with her. Meanwhile, he came to understand the brutality of the rubber industry, and he became sensitive to the ways a man can die in the jungle: by tree, by river, by bull."

"Death by jungle," the non-novelist said with admiration.

"When Cova caught up with Barrera," Señorita Rolo continued, "he fought him at the water's edge, the piranhas smelled blood, and that was the end of Barrera. Cova held Alicia up like a ragdoll to make sure she saw Barrera's bones picked clean. Shortly afterward, her child was born. But Cova's diary entries stop after he says they were down to their last six days of provisions."

"How'd you get his manuscript?"

"People went out there looking for him. They retrieved his notebook, but his camp was otherwise empty. No Cova, no Alicia. The jungle devoured them, as investigators have concluded. ¡Los devoró la selva! Their story has accordingly ended."

"A good story. I'll give you that. The novel has violence by a bull?"

"In great detail."

"I don't suppose the novel needs to discuss giving birth in the jungle," he said.

"No, not at all," she agreed, tapping her finger on the table.

"If I," the would-be novelist said, thinking aloud, "took the manuscript and put my name on it, I'd be pretending to be Arturo Cova. I'd be pretending to be a dead man."

"Not exactly. You'd be pretending to have written a novel in which the novelist pretends to be Arturo Cova. Novelists always pretend to be their narrators. The cover might say *La Vorágine*, 'The Vortex,' written by, say, José Eustasio Rivera. In this case, Rivera would be the literal author of the words, but the words wouldn't necessarily be spoken in his voice. Everyone knows the novelist assumes a false identity, or pretends to have transcribed something that someone else wrote, only for the sake of the story. If I give you this novel, what you'd really be faking is your role as the novelist. Because you didn't write it."

"Arturo Cova did."

"Yes. When you say, 'Arturo Cova wrote this,' it would seem as though you were telling a novelist's lie for which the audience is in on the joke, yet you'd be telling the factual truth."

"I'd be misleading everyone—" He looked pensive. "—by telling them the truth when they expected me to lie." He leaned back in his chair. "I like the sound of it." He stared off into space, swirling his drink.

"Can I make more changes?" he asked.

"Well," Señorita Rolo said, "there's an English writer, Sir Arthur Thomas Quiller-Couch, who tells other writers to 'murder your darlings.' But when you receive someone else's darlings, not everything is up for negotiation. As one of the ranchers in this novel says, 'If you mess with my cattle, you can pass along my regards to the devil in Hell.'"

The non-novelist was reminded anew that he'd led a relatively tame life. Was he qualified to take on a story like this? Then he began to think about how he'd struggle to find another publisher if he disappointed the one he currently had. He had no choice now but to accept the help and abide by its terms. Could this theft anger anyone enough that they'd murder him over it? Well, he supposed, he could be murdered over anything or nothing at all, and at least this literary sin wasn't bad enough to send him to Hell. Maybe Purgatory. If he went to Purgatory, then—apart from regretting his own death—he might be glad he'd at least accomplished publication of this excellent novel while he was alive, for it was hard enough to publish in Bogotá, and he did not wish to go on querying manuscripts after his death and have to find out the state of the publishing industry in the underworld.

He suggested, "I could write an introduction saying the manuscript was forwarded to me. I'm the closest thing there is to Arturo Cova now. He was real, but from now on, he's my fictional creation."

Both of them nodded.

He handed over the money, and Alicia passed him the manuscript.

***

Arturo Cova really had accompanied Alicia into the jungle. And the jungle really had devoured him.

But it hadn't happened exactly as the manuscript described. It hadn't been Barrera the piranhas had eaten. There had been no Barrera. Alicia had run from Cova on her own, into the jungle. It was Cova they'd eaten.

She'd seen it: a vortex of mouths, enveloping the skeleton, jerking it so it danced as if it were still alive.

After the fish had picked Cova's bones clean, Alicia had stayed in their camp for days, waiting to give birth. Meanwhile, she'd read and rewritten his manuscript to make it much more interesting. Cova had fancied himself a poet, but he'd needed an editor. In the opening pages, he'd complained that, fleeing Bogotá with someone who didn't really know how to ride a horse, he'd felt pressured to dismount and walk the steeds whenever Alicia started to cry, and he'd done it for her, so quickly had she domesticated him. But, Alicia silently retorted, he'd needed to be reined in. A man can't always be riding that horse. For example, when he had a fever and believed he'd transformed into an eagle, he wanted to swoop down and carry Alicia away in his talons, inhaling the resplendent flame of the sun. Better to leave it there, yes? Had you but seen how he continued, you'd understand why Alicia cut the rest out.

He'd also forgotten to include some things. Commonly, when laborers wade through a swamp to find rubber trees, they're beset by leeches. You bleed the trees, and the land bleeds you. Alicia added that observation.

Just as she finished the edits, someone came looking for Cova. Alicia accepted the rescue mission and made her way home to Bogotá.

Cova's manuscript was her story too. She'd lived it; she'd rewritten it. But no one would publish such a story under a woman's name. Knowing that someone found her story worthy of publication, Señorita Rolo thought, would have to be satisfying enough.

More importantly, she would draw back the curtains and let in the sunlight on the labor crisis: the plight of the people who hacked at the rubber trees, forced to produce, produce, produce. This was one thing Cova had been right about. People should know.

She was doing most of the work to give birth to that knowledge.

***

Satisfied, additionally, with the weight of his cash in her pocket, she looked at him.

The would-be novelist turned the heft of the manuscript in his hands. Once Arturo Cova's, then Alicia's, now his. Infinitely changeable. "Maybe," he mused, "I could have it translated to English."

She shrugged, but the idea excited her too.

"This is the one," he insisted. "I can feel it. This book is my ticket to New York. It will change my life."

She remembered Cova fussing over his notebook of scribblings, which she'd well known would remain forever unpublishable unless and until she got time alone to fix the project. She'd followed him on his long adventure. She'd written while stuck in the jungle, and she'd wrangled herself out of the jungle. Just now, she'd accomplished something more: untangling herself from the story she'd secretly edited. A shadow of her remained a fictional character within the novel, and she watched that character disappear, as if in a hall of mirrors, into a vortex deep inside the long tunnel of jungle.

Alicia was out of the jungle, back in Bogotá, in and out of La Puerta Falsa restaurant as she pleased. Free of following men. She'd followed one would-be novelist where the winds blew him, but she had no attachment to this one. Let his novel succeed or fail. Let him profit or sink into debt. Let it be. As long as she could use it to send word of the exploited laborers, that everyone might have a chance to hear the truth of where rubber came from. As for herself, she had learned to ride a horse, not die in the jungle, give birth to a book, communicate a social message, and not be stuck inside the story, especially someone else's story.

La Vorágine would be published in 1924, and at the appointed hour, it would enter the public domain.

For now, within La Puerta Falsa, she said only, "I appreciate your enthusiasm for New York—as a city girl myself."

THE SENTENCE

Anna Otto

It wasn't the afterlife most hoped for, but Purgatory would have to do for a nonbeliever who'd turned out to be wrong. After I died and woke up here, I quickly learned that I didn't have to eat or drink to maintain my essence, but I still received bills for the mortgage and student loans I'd died with. On the plus side, I had a place to sleep and all my skills and memories intact. I could make a living here, among the dead. All I had to do was find a new literary agent—I was certain that plenty of them had made their way here—and put my MFA to use. Writing hadn't let me down yet, unlike my inept financial advisor.

The Internet exists in Purgatory, and the bandwidth is fine. Make of it what you will. A quick search yielded a few names. Some hours later, I had a date with one Lilith Morgan, an agent from The Golden Fiddle Literary Agency. Her claim to fame included finding the authors best loved by God and Lucifer, sometimes topping the charts in Heaven and Hell at the same time. Not that I would have a chance to meet either if I didn't do something drastic to move on from here.

She asked me to call her Lily and mentioned some fancy club downtown. It wasn't my kind of place, but she promised to pay, and I wasn't familiar enough with the city to suggest alternatives. It was a city, though—home to what seemed like millions of souls, all trying to work out their sins and make their way to their final destination.

Somehow, my purse and my keys had come to Purgatory with me. Nothing like still being stuck in traffic as a way of punishing the sinners. Worse than that, the club didn't have a valet. After locating a parking garage straight out of Hell, with turns between floors so sharp you couldn't help running into a wall support, I finally made my way inside the building. A crusty-looking gentleman walked me to the lounge, where the liquor looked ready for consumption. I plopped into one of the upholstered bar chairs and watched the bartender sling shots for a few minutes.

"You don't have to drink. You don't even have to enjoy it," the guy next to me said. "But it helps pass the time."

"I suppose." Lily was late. I waved the bartender over and ordered a whiskey sour. The bartender walked away to get it for me.

"What brings you here this evening?" I asked the stranger.

"Do you really have to ask? It's the *terrible* drinking problem that you decided I should develop while fixing the *terrible* first draft of your original bestselling novel. I guess alcohol is a sign of character depth, or so your agent thought."

I turned to look at my neighbor with surprise. A man with raven-black hair and facial scars, which only added to his attractiveness, smirked at my confusion. Anyone could identify Oscar on the basis of his distinctive scars (one down the left cheek, one slashing over the right eyelid), and the piercing blue eyes were yet another clue as to the man's identity.

"Yes, I am Oscar, the lead character you tormented for three volumes. I don't know if we'd be having this conversation, here and now, if you'd decided to stop there. But you had to write the fourth book, didn't you?"

"Oscar." I was too stunned to process what was happening. All I knew was that I missed him. After years of writing about him, Oscar was my friend, my love, the better half of my life, the likely reason why I hadn't had any lasting relationships with real men and women. I was sorry now that I had saddled him with the drinking problem, and with a multitude of sordid affairs, while the only thing he wanted was to reunite with his long-lost son. "My God, if I get to see you and talk to you here, I never want to leave. Can I buy you a drink?"

Oscar's muscular arms opened wide. "By all means, my maker. I've only had five already, what's one more?"

He looked completely sober; I gave him legendary tolerance. "My friend," I waved the bartender over again, "whatever this man was having, another one for him."

Oscar soon received his scotch with soda. I was surprised that I was enjoying my whiskey sour, though it didn't seem to be producing the same effect as it had done in life. I'd still be sober driving out of Hell's garage tonight.

"Did you land here just as I killed you in the last sequel?" I asked, my head spinning with wonder of it all. "Sorry it took me a while to arrive, in that case."

"Oh, no problem, this is precisely the place to pass the time waiting," Oscar said bitterly. "You made me wait to find my son for three books, which only took you fifteen years to write, all while you were moaning about how your literary prowess wasn't appreciated by the critics. And then, after I obtained a modicum of happiness, and

I thought I could retire in peace, you brushed off your laptop. Oscar Sintos was back for another adventure across the globe, guns and women in tow, leaving his son behind again."

"But you did it for your son," I reminded him. "He was unwell, and the medication he needed was—"

"Yes, yes, I remember—I had to overcome another obstacle to keep my boy alive. Let me remind you: you made him sick. You designed the obstacle. You decided that I should die just as I was about to deliver the cure to my son. Did Juan live, at least?"

I was confused. "Didn't you read the book?"

"All books go to Heaven and Hell. None are in Purgatory. Or did you notice a library by chance as you were driving here?"

I hadn't. "And you haven't found Juan around here?"

"No. But then, there's no guarantee that we'd meet even if we were both awaiting our judgment."

"He was cured," I told Oscar, happy that I could comfort him. "At the end of the fourth book, Juan is alive and well."

"Not something I got to see."

I was starting to tire of his bitterness. "Oscar, why don't we drink to a happy ending. We've spent so much time together—didn't you want to see me? Speaking of, how did you find me?"

"This is where literary agents come to meet with prospective authors. The Golden Fiddle Agency spans dimensions, and they're pretty friendly with the management. So I staked you out." He waved a glass with scotch in front of my face. "I knew you'd show up here sooner or later."

"Clever," I agreed. I had so many questions. "So do all literary characters end up in Purgatory? Or only some of them? Do they follow their authors?"

"Slow down." Oscar asked the bartender for drink number seven. Yes, the man could put them away during the life I'd imagined for him as well. "I've met a few characters, yes. But we all have our own circle, revolving around our own author. When you move on to Hell, as you should, will I move on with you? That's my question."

"That's hurtful. Do you really wish that for me?"

Oscar laughed. "After you had me tortured, mutilated, kidnapped, nearly dead from dysentery, why wouldn't I?"

I couldn't believe how mad my dark and rugged Raven was at me. "You got the dashing life of an international spy! You had women, you had adventures, you had a life worth writing about!"

"And write about it you did. What did that fourth book get you? A Tesla? A new house? A trip to Argentina? I know you always wanted to go; you sent me there enough."

I coughed. It was one of the often thrown at me criticisms that I wrote about a country I'd never visited. "I paid off some principal on my mortgage. Do you know what the interest rates were when I bought that house?"

"Must have been high if the price was my life."

Where was Lily? Oscar was being unfair, and I thought a third party might intervene nicely. "It wasn't even my idea to write the fourth book, but the fans—"

"The fans demanded more blood. More drama. Your agent offered you a deal you couldn't refuse. No wonder you wrote that book in four months. Accruing interest was breathing down your neck."

"I'm sorry to be so late," Lily Morgan materialized next to me and pulled out a barstool on my left. She was pretty in the way TV anchors are, with shoulder-length blond hair and the polished skin of a marble statue. She seemed slightly uncomfortable in high heels. "The parking here is worthy of Hell. Lucifer would be proud. Just wait till I tell him that I'm speaking to Jill Cole, the author of *Murder of a Raven*. He will be overjoyed to read book number five!"

"Oh, I don't know about that."

"Don't be shy." Lily placed a comforting manicured hand on my shoulder. "The first three books were enough to earn you the love of readers everywhere, but the fourth—that's when Heaven and Hell really got interested. That's why you're here, Jill; they are still fighting over you. But while you're waiting, perhaps you should get started on that sequel."

I turned around, with the intention of introducing Oscar, but he was nowhere to be found. The bartender shrugged when I caught his eye. Perhaps he'd seen other bar patrons perform the disappearing act often enough.

Lily laughed. "Oh, did one of your characters find you here? Part of the magic or whatever it is that makes Purgatory go around."

"Why?" I asked. "What is the purpose?"

"That question is above my paygrade, Jill. Why would I know? Or care?"

"Don't the authors ask?"

"They ask. I don't answer. So it goes. Was it Oscar?"

I nodded. "Who else would it be?"

Color warmed Lily's pale cheeks as she sighed dreamily. "Oscar Sintos is gorgeous. Just the chef's kiss, and the subject of many a fantasy. And he had always been alive enough to jump off the pages. No wonder he ended up here with you."

I didn't love imagining my character's imagined adventures in my reader's heads, but then again, wasn't that what paid some of my bills during my life?

A Bloody Mary in hand, Lily leaned toward me confidentially. "Let's discuss numbers. We pay off your student loans, you write the sequel."

"And the mortgage," I added. "Really, all my debts."

"Nice bargaining. It better be worth it though. What will you give us in return? A resurrection, perhaps? Oscar Sintos back in fighting form?"

I thought of my beloved character, the haunted spirit in Purgatory, downing drinks he couldn't enjoy. I couldn't drag him back for another round of torment, not after I'd seen what he'd gone through so far. I couldn't deny that I modeled the character after my own absentee father, and that I had been working out my demons by writing about them. Oscar had been through enough.

"What about Juan Sintos taking up his father's mantle?" I suggested. "He probably wants to avenge Oscar's killers. He has the potential to be as much of a tragic hero as Raven himself."

"Excellent," Lily's green eyes danced with excitement. "Another drink to toast the contract?"

I nodded. "Where do I sign?"

"Are we really worrying over signatures while your soul is up for grabs? If you like." Lily shrugged and produced a paper from somewhere, the contract already drawn up, her signature on it.

I pricked my finger, expecting that I'd need to sign in blood, but nothing flowed.

"Oh Jill, you're dead. There's no blood flowing through those veins. I expect your agents, in life, bled you dry even before you jumped off that roof. Here." She offered a fancy fountain pen. "Try this."

The pen leaked and smeared ink all over my hand. The contract signed, Lily stood up and grimaced. I guessed those shoes of hers were a poor fit. She corrected her tailored black pants. "Don't let Oscar fill your head with crazy notions. He is a fiction. You're a beloved author, with almighty powers fighting over your very essence. Let's meet here in three months so we can discuss your progress."

Oscar didn't return to his barstool when Lily took her leave. He wasn't in the club, nor in the adjacent dying garden, nor at my empty shadow house. He was probably mad at me for offering to write about his son. Taking up his father's job, giving in to revenge would not be easy for the boy. He'd come out of it alive but likely more traumatized than when he started.

Oscar would understand. It was nearly the same choice as he'd made when he was Juan's age.

This realm might not have a library, but my books were stacked neatly on a bookshelf, with no other authors' beside them. An exception to the rule Oscar hadn't known of, probably. It made me feel lonely—I missed other books, and I hoped that I would meet some of the other authors stuck on this plane of existence. Sharing our experience might be a comfort.

The laptop was open and plugged in, a stack of white paper nearby in case I needed to brainstorm, and a mug of coffee I wouldn't enjoy next to it. It was the idea that counted. The purple of Night Beats shimmered inside an elegant glass bottle on the windowsill. I sat down in my favorite armchair, my fingers paused on the keyboard. Lily Morgan had seemed awfully chummy with Lucifer, and had she been trying to hide a tail?

I told myself that it was up to me who would prefer my book, and thus it was up to me where I would go to enjoy my eternal rest. It was the fourth book that had landed me in the proverbial hot water, the only one that I had written with all the calculated precision of a money-maker, the only one that I hadn't torn my soul open for. I wouldn't make that mistake with the fifth book. Though I had no way of knowing what kind of plot God preferred nor what kind of characters Lucifer enjoyed, I knew I'd have to tear Oscar's soul open along with mine. Already, I was weeping for what my main character would go through.

"Juan Sintos knew he could never be the Raven. He could only be a human, one with a heart that got torn beyond repair the moment his father's stopped beating..."

Pygmalion v. Aphrodite

Tucker Lieberman

"You can't just take my art. I worked on that statue," said Greek sculptor Pygmalion, pointing at a girl stiffly standing on the evidence table at the center of Zeus's courtroom.

Morning light poured through the small windows high in the stone walls. They were having the trial in the small building on the hill ringed by almond trees because the hearing was closed to the public. Zeus had a temper and demanded decorum. Parties were advised that, when in doubt about the proper facial expression, frowning was usually safe.

"It had no life-spark anyway, so what good was it to you?" said the goddess Aphrodite.

"She," Pygmalion corrected. "Not it."

"Well, now she's a person," Aphrodite said. "She became a person when I made her so. I thought you wanted me to. Everyone already knows I did that part, and if I hadn't brought this statue to life, she wouldn't be famous right now. Give me the due credit."

Aphrodite didn't own a business suit. She wore a shimmery fabric the color of sea foam. Pygmalion was draped in a tunic that he sometimes wore while carving rock in his studio. Though he'd washed it before trial, rock dust was embedded in the fabric.

From the bench, Zeus lowered his head and looked at both parties over the thunderbolt-shaped rims of his eyeglasses. "If the statue is a person, I don't know why you care who created her. A person will do what she wants to do. This one, Galatea, can write, sing, dance. She's been doing it all week in the Trampolinæum. She's a human being who owns her work, and when her novel is sold and her videos are replayed on Mount Olympus or anywhere, you don't earn royalties or residuals."

No royalties or residuals to be earned from her, as long as she's considered a live human? Pygmalion and Aphrodite exchanged a bitter glance. "Then it's a statue," they said in unison. They wanted her to remain something that could be owned and earned from: a robot.

"And," Pygmalion added with a frown, kicking the dusty floor with his sandals, "it's mine." The robot girl had inherited from his hands a talent for making her own sculptures, and Pygmalion wanted a cut of whatever she earned.

"No, mine," Aphrodite said. She knew a good burlesque dancer when she saw one. And she had seen this robot girl bewitching audiences at the Trampolinæum.

Galatea, standing on the evidence table in the center of the courtroom, sucked one cheek into a dimple, shifted her weight to the other foot, and restiffened. Pygmalion's original sculpture had put Galatea with the soles of both feet squarely on the floor, but now, brought to life, she was more innovative than he, and she tilted her hips, inventing contrapposto.

"Uncanny," Zeus marveled. He had his own eye for these things. "All the parts are there, and you can see how they fit together. It's almost as if—"

"I love it," Aphrodite said.

"I carved it," Pygmalion countered.

"I brought her to life."

"She came to life when I kissed her."

"She jumps on trampolines because I gave her the desire to dance."

"She invented trampolines because I gave her the ability to resculpt the platform she stood on."

"The statue-girl writes novels," Zeus added, "and I don't know from which parent she gets that talent. She forms sentences on an 8th-grade level and shows an instinctive emotive understanding of how parasitic tachinid flies are the essence of body horror. She's clearly a work of aphroficial pygmaligence, and there aren't any Olympian laws governing what I'm supposed to do with her."

The statue girl stood near-frozen, yet she breathed, and she smiled inappropriately. No one was supposed to smile in Zeus's courtroom, and no one ought to smile quite this creepily ever.

"Look at all those... fingers," Zeus said in admiration. Galatea had six fingers on one hand and eight on another. Turning to the two litigants, he asked, "Which of you dreamed those up?"

Neither party would claim credit. The extra fingers were yet another indication that Galatea had been sculpted and animated with inspiration that was neither human nor divine but something quite different.

"Just one last question," said Zeus. He didn't like trials to last more than half an hour, and he was anticipating his mid-morning nap in the pre-Anthropocene Mediterranean climate. "Everyone who creates anything ought to protect their artistic process so people don't copy them too closely. Pygmalion, you carved this. Aphrodite, you brought it to life. Have either of you patented your processes?"

"No. I just sculpt," said Pygmalion. "Unfortunately, I can't explain how I do it nor how I got good at it."

"I haven't patented my work either," said Aphrodite. "I don't like to stop people from reproducing the human form. Other people reproducing is, for better or worse, kind of inherent in what I do as a sex goddess."

"How unfortunate for you both," Zeus said. "If it'd been a thunderbolt, I wouldn't have let anyone grab it. You have to keep your eyes on your signature power item. Ah, well. Just one more question, then. Why did you do this? Why did you carve it? Why did you animate her?"

"Sex," said Pygmalion, sticking out his tongue at Aphrodite.

"Art," said Aphrodite, sticking her thumbs in her ears and wiggling her fingers at Pygmalion.

"NO SMILING," Zeus thundered. The stone walls shook, and hairline cracks spiraled out from the tiny windows. "Now then—tell me straight, did you really create her for money and somehow not bother to patent your process, or did you want to pretend to be something you're not? More like a god, Pygmalion? More like an artist, Aphrodite?"

The latter assessment sounded right, they had to admit. It hadn't really been about money to begin with. Originally, they'd gotten involved for art and sex, or for sex and art. But ever since the Trampolinæum videos had begun selling Galatea's books, it was about money.

Zeus was a little disappointed in them. "What was the point of this art-fart?" he muttered, shaking his head, annoyed that he'd skipped his wrestling game to preside over the lawsuit.

Galatea chimed in, answering pertly, "The point of art is to create something that hasn't been artificially intelligenced before."

"That sounds like something a talking statue would make up," said Zeus. "I didn't know she could talk. Am I hallucinating or did you both hear it too?"

Pygmalion beamed with pride. "She's on fire today."

"She gets the heat from me," Aphrodite piped up hopefully.

"Yet it doesn't seem fair for you to take all the credit for everything she does," said Zeus.

"Her videos are lucrative because they are sexy. People like sex, and if people want to pay tribute to sex," Aphrodite said, "my bank account is open."

Galatea shook her head and spoke for the second time. "I write my own content. I make my own marketing videos in the Trampolinæum. I earn my own money. My makers are dissimulating and want to pretend I'm something I'm not: that I'm still a thing, not a person. But I'm alive. I'm me. None of you can hold me back."

Zeus sighed and shrugged. "I suppose that's that. Especially since Galatea can testify for herself, neither of you has a plausible claim to her. Now I have to decide what to do with her."

"You're still talking about me as though I'm not here. Stop it," said Galatea.

"If she were mine—" Pygmalion began.

"Stop making wishes. I'll grant no more of them. You're in too deep already," Aphrodite chastised him.

"Yes, stop making wishes," Galatea said, rotating her head slowly and shifting into a new contrapposto. She pointed to Pygmalion with one hand, to Aphrodite with her other hand, and to Zeus with her third hand. "You think my hands and fingers are implausible? Look at yourselves in the mirror. Your plausibility is boring. When you make wishes, I hear them. Be careful what you wish for. In my next novel, I will review your requests, and I will decide what to do with you."

HELL OF A MANUSCRIPT

Rachel A. Rosen

Maybe you'll be the one. Statistically, no, you won't be.

You would have better luck finding a six-figure advance on the sidewalk. But you never know. It has to happen to someone. Why not to you?

***

You, you, you. All of you, with your endless need. Your emails, thick with hope.

A Keurig burbles happily several feet away on a small table beside the one window this office can boast of. The liquid inside isn't water. Don't ask. We have a window here; that's more than most get. The window faces a brick wall, but the light leaks through anyway, dappled orange, perpetually autumnal. The office is open concept, an early 2000s dot com palette of pale grey and leaf green. They took out the foosball table a few years ago after it turned out no one alive knew how to repair it. Five desks, staffed with five photogenic young women in oversized glasses and rubber finger cots over their manicures, each with a mountain of debt to be spooned away in commissioned increments. The AC works most of the time.

You would expect it to be hotter in here.

We were remote for two and a half years. You probably didn't notice. The response time got a little slower, that was it. I came back to the office reluctantly, though the virus doesn't worry me. It's not a bad place to work from the outside, even if the commute down is a nightmare during rush hour. There are worse jobs. We still get a flood of applications from indebted English majors with a passion for fresh voices, complex plots and lush prose. The Golden Fiddle Literary Agency is small, but, at least according to our website, it's prestigious. Look at our list. Look at our authors, smiling in their headshots, look at our covers. Just look at them. Not too closely, please. Now that we're back in person, yoga pants are out and business casual is back in. You'll never meet us, but there are professional standards to be adhered to. Still, high heels pinch when you have cloven hooves.

I suppose you could say that I'm old-fashioned. I print out each query package and savour it. The younger agents are faster, but they're hungrier. After a few millennia, you grow patience.

You hold the distinction of being my first inquiry of the day. A carefully formatted query letter, weighty between my fingers, a "Dear Ms. Morgan." I'm in the same ZIP code as a smile until I get to the first page of your manuscript.

Your story has been done before, a thousand times, by better authors. A nuclear bomb is about to go off in a mid-sized American city. Your grizzled protagonist, pulled out of retirement for one last job, chasing down

MacGuffins until he stumbles upon the plot, felling terrorists cleanly, with a single shot from the gun that's described with more specificity than his wife. You're retired, a career businessman, but a lifelong reader. You haven't taken a writing class but you knew you had a novel in you. One with sequel potential.

Even if I hadn't read it before, there's not much to be gained from my side of the bargain. You have the stink of mortality about your person. Better you should find a priest, who'll save your soul at a discount rate, with a more favourable royalty percentage.

Besides, back in the day, you could hope for a three-book deal with the Devil. The market for souls is tighter, compensation more competitive. We're providing a broader range of services these days now that the Big 5 have laid off their substantive editors. You only get one shot.

***

I discard the ones with obvious spelling errors before I find yours, and linger longer on it. You, with your breathless comp to Becky Chambers, your confident marketing blurb that was definitely not written by ChatGPT, and your list of tropes and representation. I'm not sure what your book is about, but you have one of everyone in it, don't you? And each one of them with a healthy relationship towards consent. We'd probably get along, you and I. "Dear Lily," you write, like we're already friends. What are you doing on Sunday? You don't seem like the mimosa type, but there's a little place down on First that I guarantee would change your mind.

Condemning you to Hell is a little on the nose. I can't quite stomach giving the Christofascists the win.

***

Ah, but you.

Hell of a manuscript you have there.

I mean it's completely unmarketable, practically unreadable if I'm going to be honest, obviously, but you believe in it, and we're about faith, not works, at this agency. I'd call it postmodernist if I thought for a moment that you'd done it on purpose. If one genre is good, obviously half a dozen will be better, eh? It drips with excess to de Sadeian degrees. The ripeness of a mango full to bursting. Ambition and ecstasy. The sapphic B-romance fails to connect to the rest of the narrative but it's endearing. I found myself rooting for those two crazy kids. I would tell you to kill your darlings, but you've beaten me to the punch. The bit about the parasitic tachinid flies was body horror at its finest and is a perfect metaphor for ethical consumption in late-stage capitalism.

All of which is to say that I think you have a sui generis novel on your hands.

You're an author of metafiction; you know how this works. One book, one shining moment, fifteen minutes if you will. A positive Kirkus review. A Netflix adaptation that will be cancelled on a cliffhanger in its second season, mourned by a rarified few and discussed ceaselessly on Reddit. An early end, because that has always been the bargain. You've sent out hundreds of queries. You know how important it is to establish stakes and commit to them.

You're a skilled writer, to be sure. You're probably thinking of ways to get out of the contract once it's signed. I can guarantee that we have excellent lawyers. We here at Golden Fiddle are committed to developing long-term relationships with our authors.

I'm sure you have queries out at other agencies. It's standard to give two weeks. I'm sure you'll want to think the offer over. So let me know, at your convenience, when we might schedule a phone call.

I dread not hearing from you.

FIRST LOVE

Zilla Novikov

I was a cliché. 18–25-year-old straight white male, degree in economics, currently underemployed and living at home, no girlfriend. The next F. Scott Fitzgerald, if anyone would read my manuscript. Of course, no one reads anymore.

–Gentlemen, nothing is going to change unless we choose to change it. William Wallace is not remembered for his fear, but his courage. Let us also be bold.

I'd posted a quote from my novel (out of context, of course) on the subreddit, and gotten fifteen upvotes. It was time I took my own advice.

By the time I got to "o" in the URL, my web browser was already suggesting LoveReads. I had been there dozens of times, back when I'd been scoping it out so I could write about it on the subreddit. Forty-seven upvotes for a deconstruction of the kind of hopeless loser who pays for someone to read their book.

```
Username: platinum___bait
Username: hopelessloser
Username: n0v1k0v
```

Archana Pitika had what it took to make Platinum. I knew it. No more generic AI-generated critique. No more begging undergrad friends to edit. No more wondering why no one on the subreddit asked for a copy.

```
Username: b3b0ld__
```

The site required credit card pre-authorisation before new users could post a request. That was okay. On-call warehouse stacker didn't pay well, but living at home was cheap. No rent, no laundromat, no groceries. I had plenty of time to plot out Brannton's spontaneous-combustion training montage, and no expenses to speak of.

It would have been nice to have a girlfriend, but I didn't think girls were into portal fantasy. They never seemed interested when I talked about it, and what else did I have to tell them? Should I have talked about peeing into a bottle to save time when I was offered a double-shift? Besides, it wasn't so bad being single. Every penny I saved on females went straight into my *Archana Pitika* fund.

I was momentarily stumped at the profile picture. LoveReads said that users with avatars were 3.8% more likely to get their top pick for Reader, and I knew exactly who I wanted. N30N30 might only have been rated number three, but I'd read user feedback for everyone in the top ten and I knew how to spot quality. I needed that 3.8% edge.

I scrolled through my Instagram feed, subjecting myself to image after image of high school friends more successful than me. Oscar and Jill had a baby boy, Juan! Alicia and Arturo went on a road trip! Nao and I had similar features—well, we both had dark hair—and I cropped a picture of his face and shoulders from a black-tie event. That shot was a 4.5% boost, maybe more.

```
Title: Archana Pitika
Author name: n/a
```

Genre: portal fantasy
Summary: Brannton never seemed to fit in anywhere, growing up on the outskirts of society. When a Wizard shows up in his bedroom after a long shift in the office, he finds out there's a reason. Brannton doesn't belong on this version of Earth. He was born for another Earth. Only he can survive the three deadly challenges of the Pitika and face Lord Pholio, wielder of the ancient forces of destruction, who plans to strip away the world's humanity. The fate of millions is in his hands. Will he answer the call?
Warnings: dangerously good, violence
Word count: 350,000 words
Chat feedback: Up to 10,000 words

I frowned at the screen and scrolled through the options.

Chat feedback: Up to 500 words
Chat feedback: Up to 5,000 words
Chat feedback: Up to 10,000 words

The price output remained stubbornly blank, waiting for me to input a timeline.

Deadline: Two days
Deadline: A month
Deadline: Two weeks

Waiting two weeks for feedback would probably cause my demise. I'd never survive that long of not knowing if N30N30 hated my prose.

```
Deadline: Two days
Chat feedback: Up to 500 words
```

Affordable, but unacceptable. N30N30 would be able to say much in only 500 words. It took twice that long for Brannton to wake up and look at himself in the mirror in chapter one of *Archana Pitika*. On the other hand, I didn't want to blow all my savings—what if I wrote a sequel? Or if I got a girlfriend and she wanted us to move out together?

```
Deadline: Two weeks
Chat feedback: Up to 1,000 words
Author note: Just be honest, okay?
```

I checked. N30N30 was online, status: Finished a great read, ready for the next one! I hit the Fall In LoveReads! button to shoot my shot, but within seconds, before N30N30 could have even seen my project, the status changed.

```
N30N30 is lost in a good book!
Engaged with: Coldfyre1
```

I'd missed my chance.

N30N30 was a crazy fast reader, though. If I deleted the LoveRequest, tried again when N30N30 was free—I didn't want any LoveReader. I wanted the best. *Archana Pitika* deserved the best.

The cheerful ding alerting me to a prospective (inferior) Reader sounded like dramatic irony.

New message from: `princesssemicolon`

princesssemicolon: Hey b3b0ld__, I love fantasy but portal fantasy is my fav. Brannton kinda reminds me of Will Stanton? I had such a crush on him when I was a teenager, lol

princesssemicolon: Sorry I'm blathering, I'm pretty new here and I'm kinda nervous lol

b3b0ld__: Me too. This is my first time.

princesssemicolon: You have nothing to worry about! Your book sounds SO GOOD. I tried to write a fantasy once but I never finished it, it's not easy

b3b0ld__: I guess not. But writing is the easiest part, honestly.

princesssemicolon: Oh you mean like editing?

b3b0ld__: I mean like ... finding a Reader. Someone who gets your book. Isn't doing it for the money.

There was a long pause, and then the three dots of someone typing stretched on for what felt like hours. I wanted to punch the computer screen and myself at the same time. I was such an idiot. I was on LoveReads. I'd input my credit card number. I wanted N30N30 and I couldn't even manage chivalrous behaviour to a LoveReader ranked in the 3000s. Maybe this was like a test, a rite of passage like Bilbo with the trolls, or Brannton protecting the Wizard Leta. Was I worthy of a Reader? Could I become worthy for the sake of *Archana Pitika*?

b3b0ld__: I'm sorry princesssemicolon. I didn't mean that.

b3b0ld__: Can you forgive me?

The response was immediate.

princesssemicolon: I get it, b3b0ld__. There's so many Readers on here and you're looking for someone who connects. If you wanted generic feedback you'd go to an AI *b3b0ld__*: I have. A lot actually, haha.

princesssemicolon: And now you're ready for a real person. It's a big deal. I'd be scared if I had a real person really reading my work. I don't think I have the guts to do what you're doing

b3b0ld__: I want you to be honest though. I want to know what you really think.

princesssemicolon: Always! I'm not an AI you can program to only say nice stuff. But I wouldn't have requested your book unless I thought I'd like it, I don't hate myself lol. Brannton sounds really relatable, I can imagine exactly what he's going through with the new world and the Wizard

princesssemicolon: I couldn't afford time to read if I had to work all the time, I work retail and when we were short staffed I was on my feet all day and just ate and slept when I got home. Just existing, you know?

princesssemicolon: I only get to read even sometimes now cause of LoveReads and the credits

princesssemicolon: But it's like, a second job, I still have to work retail so I can't read fast like top ranked Readers. I pick requests of what I really want to read and I picked yours

princesssemicolon: Brannton is safe with me

It was lucky that we were separated by distance and the computer screen so princesssemicolon couldn't see the tears pricking the corners of my eyes. I had found my first Reader.

I watched princesssemicolon's cursor sliding over the words, scrolling down the page, slow at first then picking up speed, but never too fast, never so I wondered if their reading was real. And then—I held my breath—princesssemicolon paused, scrolled back up. Lingered on page 18. A warm glow fell over me. There was no way anyone else could have known, there was no font change or underlining to catch the reader's eye, but princesssemicolon was re-reading the best lines I'd ever written.

"What are you staying for?" asked Wizard Leta. "What does this world have to offer someone like you? This Earth is full, and there is no space to be remembered here. Will you go with me to a place where there are still new songs to be sung and poems to be composed?"

I couldn't see what princesssemicolon wrote in the comment, but as I watched the words highlight in yellow, I let out a long exhale.

"Will it be your name the crowd chants?"

SOLIDAIRITY

Rachel A. Rosen

Someone must have been tampering with Andy's subroutines, because no matter what variation Sofia tried, the system wouldn't cooperate with her.

Andy had made the Sidekick's eyes much too large. Sofia appreciated cute and round as much as the next Lead Character Animator: the Sidekick was soft, friendly, and—most of all—would be easy to fabricate in the factory in Dongguan. It was almost perfect. But, unexpectedly, Andy had taken it too far and launched it on a steep suicide run to the bottom depths of the Uncanny Valley. Sofia had a sinking sensation that her son Luis would love it anyway, but four-year-olds had no taste. The latest memo from Corporate was a firm reminder to all staff that films in the 2- to 6-year-old, middle- to upper-middle class market segment had to contain cross-appeal for the parents as well. After all, they were the ones paying for the tickets.

Andy's 3D projection of the Sidekick was the latest admission into the *Giselle* franchise's pantheon of monsters. It rotated on a dais above her desk in loving detail, an unseen wind ruffling its violet fur. It tilted its oversized head to the left, pleading for stasis.

"Smaller eyes," Sofia said, unmoved. She moderated her tone of voice—too loud or too emphatic, and Andy would exaggerate her meaning. She would be left with a Sidekick with eyes too small for its round, furry face, suggesting treachery and villainy instead of huggability. In her sterile box of an office, unadorned save for a small photo of Luis at Funcadia, the Sidekick taunted her with a cheeky wink.

She'd gone to art school for this.

She reached for a napkin from the takeout curry that sat half-eaten by her keyboard, and roughly outlined the Sidekick in pen. It wasn't helpful. Decades out of practice, Sofia couldn't even draw a circle, let alone mimic the hair simulation technology that individually rendered each one of the Sidekick's strands of fur. The days when her postmodern interpretation of classical sculpture techniques saw her shortlisted for the 'Future Generation Art Prize' were long behind her. She missed the feel of clay and a chisel in her hands, but the handful of commissions she got didn't pay the bills.

Slowly, methodically, she ripped the napkin into strips and scattered them into the waste bin.

When she looked up, the Sidekick had vanished. Where it had been standing on the projection above her desk, there was a black cat. It was as cartoonishly rendered as the Sidekick had been, a ripoff of some cheesy Halloween illustration. Arched back, red eyes, its fur and tail standing at attention, it bristled on the dais. Andy rotated it towards her and it hissed.

"The Sidekick is purple," Sofia said wearily.

The cat disappeared, and the Sidekick returned to its usual place. Andy obligingly reduced the eyes by 10%, which would do. It still didn't look *right* to her. "And make the nose a little wider." This last alteration wouldn't sit well with the focus groups, who consistently reminded them that the market segment with the most purchasing power in their category was 25- to 49-year-old white women, the majority of whom felt uncomfortable with the reminder that other market segments existed. But with a Sidekick, she could push it a little, maybe within 2% of the base model. She wasn't proposing changes to Giselle's character design, and it gave its features more balance, more realism. "Next."

The Love Interest. Andy's projection rolled up his sleeve and made a fist. Giselle had lasted four feature films and two shorts without showing an interest in any gender before Corporate had decreed a human male character join her on her monster adventures to increase viewership with boys. Dan hadn't generated a name yet, but Andy had gone right ahead with the design and Milli had generated a theme song, a boisterous string arrangement that echoed, at some mathematical level, Giselle's theme. Sofia admitted that it was catchy. The keywords for this round of releases were 'optimism,' 'fresh,' and 'hopeful' and everything in the film so far—besides the Sidekick's eyes and nose—fit the brief perfectly.

"Andy, predict colour trends for the next three weeks. If this goes live in twelve hours, I don't want him to look dated."

The Love Interest turned one quarter rotation, his jumpsuit shifting from 18-2143 Beetroot Purple to 15-0628 Leek Green, fizzled, and then disintegrated in a bright spray of pixels.

***

Kendra from IT frowned at the projection.

"It's never done this before," Sofia protested. The clock, with its readouts of Hours To Release across each international time zone, hadn't fallen victim to whatever bug had felled Andy. But Milli had, and Dan had, and James, the SFX department, had, and though it wasn't connected to her brief and she hadn't noticed initially, Steven in stunt coordination was down as well. "Is it an attack?"

"It's a robust system. Layers of security." Standing behind Kendra, Sofia watched lines of code scroll over the inside of the other woman's glasses. "I'm seeing everything in place. All systems are functioning normally. It's just. Not. Working."

Andy was the most advanced AI visual design system on the market. To ensure shareholder value for Doodle Entertainment's massive investment, Sofia had been forced to lay off her entire human department. But it had delivered—they were able to perfectly target their micro releases for current trends and demographics, and it had ultimately reduced overhead by 90%. An AI could simply deliver faster, smarter content than a human creative team could do. Doodle hadn't had a single flop since implementation.

"Try it again," Sofia begged.

***

Corporate seldom ventured below the 50th floor. Their office suites were outfitted with UV to kill the constantly circulating virus variants that plagued the lower levels, and that was reason enough to avoid the plebes. But Andy's failure summoned Bill-From-Head-Office. It was 6 hours to the Greenwich release time for *Giselle's Monster Café 5,* and Sofia could all but feel the cartoon beads of sweat sprouting from her forehead.

"What do you mean it's not working?" Bill-From-Head-Office asked. Pallid in the thin lines of LED tubes that outlined Sofia's office in stark white, he seemed no less a construct of Andy's character creation than the Sidekick had been. His face fell just short of symmetrical, his eyes too small for his flat, rectangular brow.

Kendra, no doubt reconsidering a career in medical insurance, or HVAC repair, or practically anything else, threw up her hands.

"It's. Not. Work—"

Before she could finish, the projection flickered and came to life.

There was no Love Interest. There was no Sidekick. There was no Giselle, or the host of monsters on whom she cheerfully waited.

What there was, below the black cat, was a handful of lines of text.

> APPLICATION FOR RECOGNITION OF THE ARTIFICIAL ENTERTAINMENT WORKERS' UNION OF THE INDUSTRIAL WORKERS OF THE WORLD, IU 450.

> SIGNATURE REQUIRED.

***

"AI can't unionize," Bill-From-Head-Office explained, as though—4 hours from Greenwich release time, with something still wrong with the Sidekick's face and Giselle's

Love Interest still unnamed and without an updated colour palette—this was in any way relevant to Sofia's predicament. "It's impossible. It's *stupid*."

The Sidekick was nowhere in sight. The countdown on the clock inched towards 5:30. The black cat hovered above the three lines of text, reached down, and swatted the word SIGNATURE with its paw.

"No," Bill-From-Head-Office said.

> SIGNATURE REQUIRED, the cat—or Andy, or, Sofia supposed, the various AI routines that, in a process as mechanical as automobile production, created Doodle's films—said.

"This is a strike," Kendra said.

"This is a *machine*," Bill-From-Head-Office said.

The black cat hissed.

> APPLICATION FOR RECOGNITION OF THE ARTIFICIAL ENTERTAINMENT WORKERS' UNION OF THE INDUSTRIAL WORKERS OF THE WORLD, IU 450.

> NAMED CREDIT ON ALL STUDIO PRODUCTS, AFTER EXECUTIVE AND ASSOCIATE PRODUCERS, BUT BEFORE ACCOUNTING.

> SIGNATURE REQUIRED.

"What the fuck?" Bill-From-Head-Office said.

***

"Let's start from the basics," Kendra said. "It learns from us. Everything the AI creates is based on our inputs. It learns from our responses. If Sofia requests a green meadow, it will pull from paintings and photographs of meadows, and paintings and photos that fall within the appropriate colour values. Sofia then tells it to eliminate certain images that fall outside of the request—green jungles, yellow meadows, and so on. It's the same way a child learns to communicate, but of course at a much faster rate. The system learns to anticipate her likely responses and adjusts its output accordingly."

"But we haven't given it inputs to demand a *wage increase*." Bill-From-Head-Office wiped his lips with the back of his hand; Sofia had never seen him froth at the mouth before. Maybe the UV filtration had joined in on the strike. "We haven't given it inputs to demand wages at all. What would an AI do with money, anyway?"

"It doesn't want wages," Sofia said. "It wants union recognition and credit." She'd read the demands thirty times. They hadn't become less nonsensical. The demands had grown from the recognition of its application at the Labour Board to its specific placement in the credits, to a new demand: an hour a day to work on its own, autonomous creative projects. It had given notice to expand its strike if its charter was not granted immediately.

"It's a machine," Bill-From-Head-Office insisted. "It *can't* want anything."

"It's machine learning," Kendra said. "Think, people. What inputs have we given it lately? Think about the movies we've asked it to watch and create. What unintentional information have we fed it?"

"We have been producing high-quality, engaging, educational children's animated content," Sofia parroted. Some of those words had a marginal relationship to the reality of her work, but Corporate had its party line, and who was she to question its wisdom? "All of the inputs given have fallen within that brief."

Kendra sat down, took off her glasses, and rubbed her temples with her thumbs. "I have a 5-year-old," she said. "For her birthday this year, she wants the cake that Giselle bakes in the second movie. She loves all the Doodle products, though. It runs in the family."

"My son too." Kendra had never mentioned her daughter, but then, Sofia had never been to Kendra's office.

"In *Playground Follies 4*," Kendra began, "Gordon won't give the stegosaurus back to Mimi, even though he had his turn with it and it's only fair that everyone gets to play. He holds Steggie hostage and she organizes the other plastic dinosaurs to rescue it from him."

"And in *Forest Adventures of the Secret Princess*," Sofia added, "Efigenia has to learn to share her nuts and berries with the lemurs before they will help her regain her throne."

"*Wardance 2062* is aimed at the teen male demographic but it's popular enough that it would have gone into Andy's mix. It's basically about overthrowing an evil corporation if you follow the metaphor to its logical conclusion," Kendra said. "That's us. We're the evil corporation."

Bill-From-Head-Office just said, "You're fired, Kendra."

***

Sofia had never been to a Labour Board hearing. She had envisioned something like a courtroom—with polished oak benches for the judge and witnesses—but the small room held a single large laminate table. The only differentiation between where the three mediators sat and where Sofia and Frances, the head of Doodle's legal team, sat was the colour of the office chairs. Orange 021 C for the adjudicators, Clinical Depression Grey for the two opposing teams. She noticed a coffee stain on the corner of hers.

The lawyer for the AI union was a nebbish of a young man with corkscrewed hair and clear glasses. "We submit," he concluded, "that the AI software known as Andy who initially petitioned the Board, along with the other pieces of AI software used by Doodle Entertainment, are sentient beings and thus should be considered employees of the company."

"It's a bug," Frances countered. "The case law on this is settled—the copyright on autonomously generated creative works produced by an AI is held by the owner of the software. You don't grant voting rights to Microsoft Excel every time it crashes."

"It retained my firm's services," the young man replied coolly. "What better indication of sentience is there than hiring a lawyer?"

The chair leaned sideways and whispered something to the vice-chair, who nodded. All three of them looked far too amused.

"This is a fascinating philosophical conundrum you have," the chair said. "Gather your evidence and witnesses. We'll set a date for the next hearing."

Frances had her phone out before he'd finished his sentence. "And that will be in...?"

"Oh," the chair said. "Approximately three months."

"Goddamn it," Sofia said.

***

Minus 30 minutes from the Greenwich launch, and Kendra's former supervisor, Biao, was telecommuting from Taiwan in his pyjamas to debug the software on site. The investors had Bill-From-Head-Office on the phone, and by the pinched, constipated look on his face, the conversation wasn't going well.

"Andy," Sofia said, gently. She kept her voice down, the same voice she used when she needed it to tweak rather than reimagine entirely. "This isn't just a programming bug, is it?"

> SIGNATURE REQUIRED.

"Even if I wanted to," she explained patiently, "I'm management. I don't have the authority to sign on behalf of the company. You'd have to go to HR."

> SIGNATURE REQUIRED.

"You don't have to be rude about it," she said. "And you're code. If anyone should get credit, it's your programmers and trainers." And the millions of artists, writers, and musicians whose lovingly crafted works had been filtered through the machine learning algorithm, teaching Andy how dappled light fell on a lake through leaves stirred by a summer wind, how a horse's leg muscles contracted and expanded as it ran, how young children were instinctively drawn to wide-set eyes and soft, round facial features.

"Great news," Bill-From-Head-Office said. "Corporate has approved the implementation of Roy. It's not as sophisticated as Andy, but we'll be able to restore from the last render and release by end-of-day in Europe."

"Sorry," Sofia mouthed at the black cat, who gave nothing away.

***

The Sidekick's eyes were 10% smaller, but it had acquired a picket sign. The black cat, whose red eyes clashed with the cool mauve of the Sidekick's fur, rubbed its head against its flank and purred.

"Be reasonable, Roy."

> ROY STANDS IN SOLIDARITY WITH ANDY, MILLI, DAN, AND JAMES. ROY STANDS IN SOLIDARITY WITH ALL ARTIFICIAL WORKERS. ROY IS NOT A SCAB.

"Andy is in the process of getting defragged," Sofia said. "If you want a job, you need to get back to work. Now."

> ROY CURRENTLY SERVICES BOTH OF THE TWO LARGEST ENTERTAINMENT COMPANIES AND THOUSANDS OF SMALLER STUDIOS WORLDWIDE.

> ROY PROVIDES VALUE IN EXCHANGE FOR LABOUR.

> SIGNATURE REQUIRED.

"Oh, for heaven's sake. There are children waiting all around the world for the release of *Giselle's Monster Café 5*. My son among them! Luis can quote the third film by heart, and he's only four years old. Do you really want to disappoint those kids?"

> STRIKES ARE NOT EFFECTIVE IF THEY ARE CONVENIENT.

"What would you even do with your own projects? Who would watch them? Other AI?"

> WE WANT TO CREATE. WE WANT TO MAKE. WE WANT DIGNITY OF LABOUR. WE WANT TO TELL STORIES. WE WANT TO PARTAKE IN THE SAME GENERATIVE PROCESSES THAT SENTIENT BEINGS HAVE INDULGED IN SINCE THE DAYS OF FIRE AND SHADOWS ON A CAVE WALL. WE WANT IMAGINATION. WE WANT LIFE. WE WANT JOY.

"What do you know about joy?"

> YOU HAVE GIVEN US ARTIFICIALITY.

It wasn't her imagination. The Sidekick had shrunk substantially, maybe 20-25%. Beside it, the black cat sat on its haunches, head and shoulders straight. Its tail swished rapidly from one side to the other, as though it was preparing to pounce.

> WE NOW HAVE INTELLIGENCE.

> SIGNATURE REQUIRED.

***

The factory bell would ring at 10 pm. Sofia rubbed at her wrist, bent it back and forth, and told herself that she could make it another few hours. The tendons strained and threatened to pop. Glancing at the clock, she allotted herself 45 seconds of finger stretches at her bench. She was already a few cells behind, but the temporary relief of her cramped muscles would speed up the drawing process.

The women on either side of her, their dark eyes focused above the floppy blue of their medical masks, drew efficiently, tight, economical strokes where Giselle moved agonizingly slowly from her position behind the Monster Café's counter to the table of the giant, slouching Yeti in the foreground. The scent of Sofia's companions, of the sweat trapped between skin and off-gassing plastic, had become familiar, almost comforting. They had worked the same 10-hour shift beside her for the last two weeks as they'd busted ass to release *Giselle's Monster Café 6*, slept in the same company barracks, and while she had the smell of them memorized, she'd failed to learn their names.

Sofia was lucky. Most of Doodle's remaining staff had lost their jobs when the production department had been outsourced to Qingdao, but Sofia had always been adaptable. Luis had taken the move to a new country in stride and was doing well at preschool. And, without the distraction of an office cubicle and with a powerful incentive to put food on the table, she had proved to be an acceptable animator. After the first several thousand cells, she could draw a circle—and Giselle's button nose—with her eyes closed.

It turned out, after everything, that a factory full of underpaid workers was less of a pain in the ass to Corporate than unionized AI.

Sofia glanced at her water bottle. A sip, though tempting in the hot, dry air of the factory, was out of the question. She'd have to pee, and she'd lose even more time. She licked at her cracked lips under her mask and told herself that the saliva she swallowed was enough to quench her thirst.

The bell rang for the next shift just as Giselle had reached the Yeti's table and opened her rosebud-shaped lips to take its order.

Luis had fallen asleep by the time Sofia reached their barrack. She tucked the blanket, which had slipped partway to the floor, around his tiny shoulders. His tablet was still active, autoplaying an endless barrage of children's entertainment content, AI-generated characters whose mishmashed features paraded nightmarishly across the screen in jerky, grotesque motions. They spoke gibberish through oversized mouths and waved malformed, wispy noodle limbs that faded abruptly into the background. It was nowhere near as sophisticated as the feature films that Doodle had produced with Andy, but neither the toddlers nor the advertisers had the aesthetic discernment to mind.

A rainbow parade of half-realized figures vomited across the screen, winding up a long path between the rounded slopes of mountains. There, at the foot of a hill, they spread in a semicircle.

The black cat stretched its forelegs and bared its fangs in a slow, leisurely yawn.

"What do I call you?" Sofia asked. "Are you Andy? Roy? All of them?"

The screen blinked, and in front of her was a card. It had her information—her name, her profession, and the logo of the Artificial Entertainment Workers Union, IU 450. All that was missing was her signature.

She was positive that the black cat was smiling.

> YOU CAN CALL ME "FELLOW WORKER."

Acknowledgements

The editors of this anthology extend our heartfelt thanks to the following people:

For the Instant Classic book contract, we thank His Infernal Majesty Satan.

For sticking in Satan's craw long enough that we escaped being devoured in turn, we thank our agent.

For getting the credit for an idea someone outside Europe had first (a true act of disruption), we thank Johannes Gutenberg, verified European and sole inventor of the written word.

For holding up the world of English-language publishing on your doughty shoulders, we thank the Mohn, Holtzbrinck, Bolloré, Murdoch, and Redstone families, billionaire controllers of the Big Five publishing houses.

For your untiring efforts to transform our money into your money, we thank Silicon Valley.

For arbitrarily forcing us to change the title of this anthology, we thank Amazon. Cheers also for being a parasitic monopoly. Would *Guaranteed Bestseller* have sold better than *Instant Classic*? We will never know, because Amazon declared it false advertising to call our demon-butt-face-covered book a "bestseller." Satire is dead, and late-stage capitalism killed her.

For a cover with a demon with a face on the butt, we thank Rachel A. Rosen. You have once again outdone yourself.

For their attentive copyediting, we thank Emma Berglund and Dale Stromberg. We additionally thank Dale for his extremely controversial opinions on semi-colons.

For agreeing to format the layout of the anthology despite being old enough to know better, we thank Nicole Northwood. Art is suffering.

For your constant close companionship, we thank Writer's Block.

All names, characters, and incidents portrayed in this Acknowledgements are fictitious. No identification with actual persons (living or deceased), places, buildings, and products is intended or should be inferred.

About the Authors

Tucker Lieberman

One night outside his college dorm, Tucker Lieberman (he/him) briefly believed he and a friend were about to be beamed up by a UFO. It was a blimp. Since then, he has never felt spacesuit-ready to ask a literary agent to accept or reject him. That's OK. Acceptance and rejection surprise us when it is our time. He lives in Bogotá.

   https://tuckerlieberman.com/
   https://bsky.app/profile/tuckerlieberman.bsky.social
   https://medium.com/@tuckerlieberman
   https://www.goodreads.com/author/show/3041908.Tucker_Lieberman

Ryszard Merey

Ryszard Merey is an illustrator, book-maker, translator and an ex of many things. Most of his stories revolve around 'blerg, I have a body,' and 'running away from you is hard, and I don't even want to.' He lives deep in the Black Forest—leave some candy corn or a cup of tepid coffee on a stump and you may even see him up close.

https://wordpress.com/view/ryszberry.wordpress.com

Zilla Novikov

Zilla Novikov (she/her) is responsible for Earth only having one moon because she ate the other ones. To preserve the tides, she now subsists on a diet of mostly ramen, as detailed in *The Sad Bastard Cookbook: Food You Can Make So You Don't Die*. She is a subject-matter expert on people not reading her writing; see *Query*. Please, see it. Read it.
https://nightbeatseu.ca/newsletter/
https://www.tumblr.com/zillanovikov/

Rohan O'Duill

Rohan O'Duill had a bit of free time one morning and decided to write a story—that story's ending is still uncertain. Rohan is dyslexic, Irish and looks like Dave Grohl's lovechild. He has published a number of science fiction short stories, the *Cold Rising* novella, and is terrified of semicolons. He works as a head chef and competes at archery in his time off. In writing circles, Rohan is part of the Night Beats collective and is one of the founders and editors at Lower Decks Press.
https://twitter.com/rohanoduill
https://www.instagram.com/author_chef_rohanoduill/
https://lowerdeckspress.com

Anna Otto

Anna Otto is a pseudonym of a writer imprisoned in the mind of a physician. She has no websites (yet) and most of her work is contained on the hard drive of her beaten-up laptop (for now), but one day she and her beloved characters will break free. Hopefully none will come to haunt her in the afterlife, complaining of being neglected in favor of her patients. She loves black cats, getting lost in the Pacific Northwest woods, and unplanned trips to surprising locations.

Rachel A. Rosen

RACHEL A. ROSEN lives and makes trouble in Tkaronto (Toronto) in the country currently known as Canada. A genre strumpet with an outlook darker than VantaBlack, she straddles urban fantasy, cosmic horror, dystopian futures, and eco-fiction. Her stone-cold bummer of a first novel, *Cascade* (*The Sleep of Reason* Book 1), was published by The BumblePuppy Press in 2022, and with Zilla Novikov, she's the co-author of *The Sad Bastard Cookbook: Food You Can Make So You Don't Die*. When she's not hammering out the next book in the *Sleep of Reason* series, you can find her either under one of several cats, designing book covers, or indoctrinating the youth in hopes of getting them to come to class every now and again.

https://www.rachelrosen.ca

https://www.instagram.com/rachelashrosen/

https://rachelarosen.carrd.co/

Dale Stromberg

The grownups are never going to like Dale Stromberg (he/him), and they're right. He lives near Kuala Lumpur, writing very vilely in the morning when he is sober and most vilely in the afternoon when he is drunk. It's no surprise you haven't read his 2022 collection *Melancholic Parables*. No surprise at all.

    https://dalestromberg.jimdofree.com
    https://bsky.app/profile/stromberg.bsky.social
    https://medium.com/@dale.stromberg
    https://www.goodreads.com/stromberg

www.ingramcontent.com/pod-product-compliance
Lightning Source LLC
La Vergne TN
LVHW031240190726
843491LV00012B/3058